Rosie,

THE SECRET ON
THE SECOND SHELF

Jonathan White

Copyright © 2016 Jonathan White

All rights reserved.

Cover design by Joseph Emnace

This book is a work of fiction and any resemblance to
actual persons,
living or dead, is purely coincidental.

www.thesecretonthesecondshelf.com

First Edition
Printed by CreateSpace, an Amazon.com company

ISBN: 1537772503
ISBN 13: 9781537772509

For Katie and Ashton

CHAPTER ONE

Streams of purple, red and green fireworks exploded in the cool November evening. Tim looked up. They were now descending at an unnatural pace and colourful sparks were fanning out and darting towards him. He flinched, and, stumbling, tried to shoo them away. Just as they were about to strike he scrunched up his shoulders and squeezed his eyelids shut. Then it hit him all at once. He opened one eye, then the other, raised his hands and turned them from side to side. He was covered in multi-coloured gunge. Whatever it was, it had no smell, but there was no mistaking the fact that it looked like he had been doused with liquidised M&Ms. But instead of burning, his hands felt cold. He relaxed his shoulders and tilted his head upwards. What was this stuff and where had it come from? Was it a new type of firework or a nutter with a paintball gun taking random shots at Cambridge's finest?

A rocket exploded and he cupped his ears. The watery spray above his head, which he had assumed was made up of sparks, decelerated instantly. As he drew his hands away the spray sped up. It was the weirdest thing he'd ever seen – it was like the laws of physics had gone on strike. He brushed his jacket and rubbed his hands together, but he couldn't get rid of the colour.

'Tim, what are you doing?' asked his dad as the noise of the rocket faded.

'What do you mean what am I doing? Can't you see? I'm covered in this gunk. Some kind of paint from those stupid fireworks,' said Tim.

'What are you talking about? What paint?'

Tim looked down at his jacket, then at his hands. 'Oh, that's weird. I could have sworn...'

It was then that the sky exploded in a fountain of golds, reds and silvers. Roman candles erupted from all sides of the field, multiple high pitched shrieks followed burst after burst of white sparks, which sprayed upwards, lighting up the crowd by the hot dog stand.

Tim flinched. Rockets fizzed and shot high above the roaring bonfire, spurting clusters of coloured light, and spreading out in all directions. Bang. Bang. Bang.

He ran his hands through his hair and tried to make out what his dad was saying.

'I can't hear you,' said Tim, holding his ears, his face screwed up. He looked down at his jacket. No splashes of paint. Had he really imagined it before?

'I said,' shouted Tim's dad, 'where's your mum with those hot dogs?'

'Can't see anything from here. It's too far away, too dark,' said Tim, trying to get a fix on the hot dog stand.

'Best if you go and give her a hand. Look how busy it is. She probably can't find us.'

'I can do,' said Tim looking at his watch. 'But I'm meeting a couple of mates here in about half an hour, remember?'

Tim wasn't against keeping up their family tradition of attending Bonfire Night on Midsummer Common – which was, as his dad habitually boasted, the biggest show in East Anglia. But, like any street-savvy fourteen year old, he felt a strong compulsion to keep a safe distance from his parents.

Suddenly there was the sound of shots firing from all directions. It was like they were in the middle of a frenzied Wild West gunfight. Greens, reds, purples and blues danced high above Tim's head, gracefully dissolving into each other: purples merging with greens, reds with blues, then eventually fading into nothingness.

'I wish they'd stop letting off those bangers,' said Tim, shielding his ears. He turned to his dad, nodded and walked off. He had just reached the hot dog stand when two young boys, no older than seven or eight, jumped out in front of him.

'Hey, watch it! You'll set fire to someone with those if you're not careful,' said Tim.

The two boys looked at one another and sniggered, then the younger of the two waved his sparkler at Tim, so close that it was just a whisker away from his nose. Tim winced and took a step backwards. The older boy's face turned white, his expression gaunt. He looked up at Tim, jerking his neck to one side.

'Re-mem-ber,' he said, in a deep, croaky voice, sounding older than his years.

'What did you say?' said Tim, looking back at the boy.

The colour returned to the boy's face.

'Say? I didn't say anything,' said the boy, waving his sparkler.

'You heard him?' said Tim, looking at the younger boy.

'I didn't hear nothing,' said the boy.

'Anything,' said Tim.

The boy gawped at him.

'You didn't hear *anything*,' said Tim, shaking his head.

4

'Come on, you two,' said a loud voice.

Their mum appeared and grabbed them by their hoods.

'They're not so bad,' she said, winking at Tim.

Tim shrugged and strode off towards the hot dog stand. He walked the length of the twenty or so-strong queue. She must have got the hot dogs already. Dad was probably right. She was out there somewhere, trying to find them.

Tim passed the raging bonfire. He pulled down the zip on his coat to let in some air then wiped the sweat off his brow.

A teenager in front of him shook a can of coke furiously and tossed it into the fire. It exploded almost immediately.

Just as Tim turned his attention away from the can, a loud scream burst from the flames. A rush of air blew a scarf past the burning Guy. For a moment, the scarf seemed to be fire proof. The scream played back in his head as the scarf flared up. He turned to the Guy, and saw that its dark body was ablaze. A fragment of the jacket came away from the body and landed inches from his feet. It was charred, but still distinctly red. He looked back at the scarf, which was being shaken by the fire, heightening its blueish, purplish hue.

Red jacket. Purple scarf.

'Mum!' Tim screamed, staring at the Guy. 'Mum! It can't be..'

He scrambled to find a log and grabbed hold of one. He winced as the flames sprang out. As soon as the log touched what Tim had assumed was the Guy's head, he felt it being pulled away in short jerks, as if he were in a tug of war with some malevolent force.

'What the...?' said Tim.

He blinked uncontrollably as the log shot out of his hand, cutting the skin on his palm like a razor blade. A bird, twice the size of a crow and blacker than a shadow, shot out of the roaring fire, the log gripped tightly in its claws.

'Look out Tim, it's coming straight for you!'

Tim felt a pair of hands pull him backwards.

'Dad!' shouted Tim, as the bird rushed over his head, rising higher and higher. 'Dad, it's Mum. Something's happened. I heard her scream. Quick, we have to do something. She's on the fire, Dad. The Guy... it's Mum!'

Tim's dad rested his hands on Tim's shoulders.

'No, Tim; it's just a Guy. A regular Guy Fawkes. Have you been drinking?'

Tim wiped the tears away with his sleeve, rubbing dirt, smoke and ashes into his eyes. 'No, Dad, you've got to believe me. I heard her scream. I saw her scarf, her jacket.'

'Look, I'll just call your mum.'

Without waiting for a response, Tim pulled away from his dad and reached for a loose log.

'I can't get a signal,' said his dad.

'Dad, come on. We've got to get her off the fire. Quickly.'

'Tim, calm down. Don't be ridiculous. Give that here; it's just a stuffed dummy.'

His dad took the log from him and thrust it into the Guy's stomach.

Tim screamed. 'No, Dad, no!' He tried to grab onto the log and pull it away, but his dad yanked it free. 'You're hurting her. Get off!'

Tim's dad scooped out the mid-section of the Guy, dropped it to Tim's feet, tossed the burning log back into the fire and took hold of Tim's shoulders.

'Dad, what have you done?' Tim asked, struggling to break free.

'See Tim, it's just straw,' his dad replied. He picked up a few strands, dropped them onto Tim's hands and looked at the crowd of faces that had gathered. 'The show's over, folks. All good here.'

Tim shook his head.

'But Dad, I heard her,' he said, staring at the pieces of straw. 'It was Mum. We've got to find her.'

'Look Tim, I don't know what you think you heard. Probably that bird squawking. It was a big ugly brute of a bird, I'll give you that.'

'What about her scarf. Her jacket?'

'Show me. Where?'

Tim scouted the base of the bonfire for evidence.

'I can't see anything here now. But Dad, I'm telling you, it was Mum's scarf. Mum's jacket.'

'Come on Tim. You know how crazy that sounds. Look, your mum is out there. Let's just calm down and go look for her.'

Tim picked up a log close to the base of the bonfire and bashed it against the Guy.

'Claire!' shouted his dad.

Tim turned abruptly, following his dad's line of sight. He could only see her back, but she was clearly holding hot dogs. She couldn't have been more than twenty feet away. It was her red coat, alright. Thank God she was okay. Thank God it was just his crazy imagination acting up again.

'Hey Claire, over here,' shouted his dad.

Tim tossed the branch into the heart of the fire and sprinted towards his mum. 'Mum, where've you been? I thought...'

Tim felt his stomach turn to ice as she span around, a puzzled look on her face.

'But you're... you're not...' said Tim.

Tim gawped as the woman took a huge bite from the hot dog. Mustard slithered out of the sides and dribbled down her wrinkly chin. If Mr Grumpy had a wife, she would have looked exactly like this.

Tim's dad caught up, looked the woman up and down and sighed.

'Dad, now do you believe me?'

'Tim, your mum isn't burning on the bonfire.'

'You think I imagined her screaming?'

'Look, I'll try and call your mum again. She's just got lost in the crowd, you'll see.'

He pulled out his mobile phone and dialled "Claire".

Tim turned to the crowd and caught the eye of the older of the boys holding sparklers. The boy's head was bent awkwardly again, at forty-five degrees, and he seemed to be saying something. 'Rem. Re-mem. Re-mem-ber.'

The deepness in the boy's voice made him feel uneasy. It was like the boy had been possessed by a demon – a demon that was just learning to speak English. Remember. Remember what?

'I've got a signal now. It's just started ringing,' said his dad. 'Must be a bad connection here. Only one bar.'

Tim stared at his dad, the word "remember" spinning in his head.

'Tim, you look like you've seen a ghost,' said his dad as Sparkler Boy's head jerked back into place.

Tim reached into his back pocket and pulled out a phone. It was buzzing. 'It's Mum's phone, Dad. Why would Mum's phone be in my pocket?'

His dad stopped calling, took the phone off Tim and shook his head.

'You see. I'm not imagining it. How do you explain that?' said Tim.

'Let's not overreact Tim. I'm sure there's a logical explanation. Are you sure Mum didn't give it to you to look after?'

9

'Of course not. I'd remember that.'

'Come on, let's go and look for her.'

Outside the hot dog stand, Tim's dad looked around anxiously at all the faces in the crowd.

'Dad, I've already looked. She's not here.'

'She has to be somewhere nearby Tim. People don't just disappear like that.'

'Over there, Dad. The ambulance. Let's go and ask someone. What if she's had an accident?'

'Good thinking, come on.'

At the ambulance, they found two elderly medical workers.

Tim's dad approached one of them and asked, 'sorry to bother you, but have you treated a woman tonight? My wife. Slim. Mid-thirties, red jacket?'

'No, sorry, we've only had to deal with a nipper tonight. Burnt his hand on one of those godforsaken sparklers.'

'My son thinks he heard her scream. By the bonfire. She went to buy us hot dogs, you see.'

'How long ago was that?' asked the medical worker.

'Well, ten, fifteen minutes ago.'

'I wouldn't worry, sir. You can see how busy it is. She's probably lost. I know it's noisy, but have you tried calling her?'

'Well, that's the thing,' said Tim's dad, showing them her phone. 'We found her phone in my son's back pocket.'

'We could call Pat,' said the other medical worker.

'Who's Pat?' asked Tim's dad.

'Local police. He's on-site here. I could radio him'.

Tim's dad nodded.

'I understand that your mum's missing?' said Pat.

'That's right,' said Tim.

'Can you tell me what happened?'

Tim took them to the bonfire, where he pointed to the Guy, whose head had by now burnt clean away. 'I was standing right here. I heard a scream.'

'You saw your mum?'

'Well no, I heard her.'

'*Her* scream?'

'Yes, I already told you.'

'You're sure it was your mum?'

'I saw Mum's scarf fly out of the fire. Part of her jacket. Of course it was my mum.'

The policeman poked around the ground, scraping his feet over the burnt ashes. 'Son, do you remember where you last saw the clothes?'

'Somewhere here I think.'

'I tried calling her,' said Tim's dad, passing his wife's phone to Pat.

'And that's when I found her phone in my pocket,' said Tim. 'She never gives me her phone. So how do you explain that?'

The policeman shrugged. He held the phone close to the fire and twisted it around. 'Burn marks,' he said. 'There are burn marks on the phone.'

Tim nudged his dad. 'Hey, you're blocking the light.'

As his dad stepped aside, Tim looked closer at the phone. 'Not just burn marks. Look, they're fin-gerprints. Black finger prints.'

Pat took out a cellophane bag and placed the phone inside. 'It's probably nothing, but I'll get this looked at. Look, before she went missing. When did you last see her?'

'Well, just before she went to get the hot dogs,' said Tim.

'And when she went to get the hot dogs, what kind of mood was she in?' asked Pat.

'Look, she was just fine,' said his dad. 'Happy. This hasn't got anything to do with her mood.'

As they followed Pat towards the hot dog stand Tim felt his heart pounding, as he recalled the shriek from the fire and the big ugly bird shooting towards him. It was then that he noticed a partly burnt post-er stuck to the side of the hot dog stand. He picked it up and turned it over. It was vaguely familiar; he remembered seeing it on the school noticeboard. It was an advert for their local Bonfire Night, and it had just a few words remaining.

"Remember, remember, the fifth of November."

He looked back at the crowd. It felt like he was sinking; his stomach was tied in a thousand knots. That very moment he caught the gaze of Sparkler Boy. The boy's head cocked to one side as before, looking straight at him.

'Re-mem-ber,' said Sparkler Boy in a whisper, smirking as he turned towards the bonfire.

CHAPTER TWO

Tim picked up a photo from his bedside cabinet. His mum looked so young. Was it only a year since she'd gone missing? It felt more like a hundred. It was as if she'd been sucked out of time and space. Sometimes Tim even thought she'd been abducted by aliens. How could the police investigations fail to find a single clue as to her whereabouts? They'd traced the fingerprints on her phone to Sparkler Boy. They assumed that the boy had stolen her phone and probably placed it in Tim's pocket as a prank, but the accused swore he knew nothing about it. None of it made any sense. They even questioned his dad like a common criminal, suspecting he had something to do with it. His dad wouldn't hurt a fly. A whole year and all they had was a missing person's report. How could the police be so useless?

He sighed, putting the photo back in its place, and just then he heard the doorbell. At seven o'clock in the morning? Who on earth...

'Answer the door, Tim!' shouted his dad from the next room.

Tim sprinted downstairs and fumbled with the door latch.

A tall, middle aged man dressed in a long, dark grey coat looked up at Tim. He had a clipboard in one hand and a small package in the other.

'It's a bit early in the morning for the post,' said Tim.

'Sign here,' said the man calmly, passing Tim a pen.

'I thought it was all electronic these days,' said Tim.

The postman shrugged.

Tim signed his name, but it was a strange experience. He could have sworn that the pen was getting hotter as he did so. It was like his signature was being burnt into the clipboard.

The postman pulled the clipboard away sharply. 'This is for you, I believe, young sir.'

Tim repeated his words in his head. 'This is for you, I believe, young sir.' Who talked like that?

'Who... who is it?' called Tim's dad.

'Just the postman, Dad. Something for me,' shouted Tim towards the stairway, turning to pass the pen back.

As the postman walked away, Tim spotted that he didn't have a postbag.

'I haven't seen you before, have I?' asked Tim.

'First day,' said the postman and he strolled down the driveway, admiring the small stone fountain in the front garden as he went.

Tim scratched his head roughly, then closed the door, struggling with the latch, and returned to the warmth of the house. His gaze was firmly fixed on the parcel as he approached the bottom of the stairs.

Bang.

Straight into his stubble-faced dad.

'Hey, watch it!' said his dad.

'Good of you to join the land of the living. Now, let's see what's inside,' said Tim.

He led the way to the kitchen, then sat down on a stool by the breakfast bar.

'Put the kettle on,' said his dad.

Tim put the parcel down, lifted the kettle, shook it a little then nodded before switching it on.

'Who's it from?' asked his dad.

'Don't know. I don't recognise the handwriting,' said Tim, inspecting the parcel.

Tim's mind raced as he thought about what could be inside this curious delivery. A bomb? Surely not. They didn't have any enemies. And he distinctly remembered his dad tipping the dustbin men last Christmas.

'Is there a postmark? Can you see where it's from?' said his dad.

Tim turned the parcel over a couple of times.

'No. No postmark.'

He slid his finger in at one corner of the parcel and pulled at the sides, tugging it open. It was tightly wrapped, and the paper was hard to get through. Inside was a plain-looking cardboard box.

'Open it up then!' said his dad.

Tim spun on the stool and grabbed the first knife he could find from the kitchen drawer. He sliced the top off the cardboard box and reached inside. Hmmm... It was cold. Cold and distinctly metallic.

'What is it Tim? What's inside?'

Tim pulled out a bronze-coloured compass with a bevelled push button on its side. He pressed down the button, which felt warm. Warm and... tingly.

'Are you alright son? You've gone as white as a sheet,' said his dad.

Tim looked at the compass, then at his dad and shook his head.

'It's probably nothing. Just that I had a strange dream last night. I remember this large clock flying towards me. But now I think about it, I remember the letters N.E.S.W.' He paused. 'Of course: north, east, south, west. It wasn't a clock; it was a compass, a giant compass.'

'You're always having weird dreams,' said his dad.

'Not quite like this one. Somehow this was much clearer than before. More real. In my other dreams it's always felt like I've had water in my eyes.'

'Is there a note inside?' said his dad.

Tim felt around inside the box. Nothing. He pulled at the wrapping and turned it on all sides. His name and address were written out neatly:

Timothy Shaw
8 Crosby Street
Cambridge

He placed his finger back on the button. The lid popped open with a spring and stopped at precisely a ninety-degree angle, revealing a round mirror on the inside lid. It made a sharp hiss as it came to a stop, as though it was some kind of hydraulic system. The glass surface was clean – not a smudge in sight. Just below the silver needle Tim noticed a miniature spirit level. The bubble in the middle moved from side to side as he tipped the compass one way, then the other. When he closed the lid, he noticed that there were words etched on top.

"NATURAL SINE," they read.

He flipped the compass lid open again. Who'd ever seen a compass with eight sides? Weren't compasses meant to be round?

'Why would anyone send you a compass?' said his dad.

'Dunno,' he said. 'Maybe someone thinks I've lost my way!'

His dad shook his head.

Tim looked at the kettle, which was now boiling noisily, then started to prepare the tea. He passed his dad a cup, which his dad placed beside the compass. Then Tim noticed that the steam seemed to be being drawn towards the centre of the compass. He raised his eyebrows as the creepy, swirling steam was sucked in faster and faster. The silver needle began to pulsate with a sapphire-blue glow, making Tim think that the compass had its very own heartbeat.

He was beginning to wonder if he'd woken up at all. But before he could find an answer, the needle stopped glowing and the compass lid closed.

'It wasn't me,' said Tim's dad, raising his hands in the air.

They walked into the living room, Tim fumbling with the compass as they went.

'Christ, is that the time?' said his dad. 'I've got to go. I'll see you later, okay?'

'But what about the compass?'

'I wouldn't worry, Tim. It's obvious, isn't it?'

'Is it?'

'Yes, someone's playing a joke on you.'

'I'm not so sure,' said Tim, scratching his head.

'Look, don't worry. Someone's going to own up to it at school. You'll see. Hey, don't forget to set the alarm when you leave, okay? You remember the scare I got last week when you forgot.'

'Okay, okay Dad.'

His dad grabbed his coat and left the house.

Tim ran upstairs and placed the compass on the corner of his desk. He pulled out a tray of paints, flipped on an overhead light and started preparing a thick sheet of canvas paper. Almost instinctively, he rested the tip of his favourite paint brush on his lower lip, then began to paint.

A screech from outside made Tim jump, accidentally smudging the canvas with his brush. He spun around towards the window on his swivel chair, then got up, lifted the latch on the window and opened it as far as it would go.

The street lights were dim and obscured by the skinny trees that lined the street. He scanned his front garden and noticed the green wheelie bin was lying on its side.

All Tim could hear were creaks and groans from the trees outside, swaying in the early morning breeze. He shrugged and returned to his painting. He became completely absorbed in his work, only returning to reality when his alarm clock came to life again, announcing that it was eight o'clock.

Shower, breakfast, school.

He skipped to the bathroom and flipped on the shower.

＝⊹ ⊹＝

Tim darted out of the house clutching a bagel. He had almost got to the end of his front garden when he heard a rustle in the hedge.

There it was again. Louder this time. Nearer. He listened, but there was nothing but silence.

Taking a deep breath, he blew out his bagel and cheese vapours into the cold December air and brushed the crumbs off his coat.

His phone buzzed and he flipped it open.

"New message."

It felt like someone had stuck a big syringe in his arm and drained the blood from his body. He mouthed the words slowly as he read.

"Do you want to know what happened to your mother?"

CHAPTER THREE

What kind of sick joke was this? An image of Tim's mum appeared in his head. He skipped to "messages received" and tapped "view sender".

"Blocked. Unknown."

He turned from side to side and was about to reply when...

Buzz.

Another text message.

"Follow the compass when you see the light."

Was this for real? Who was sending these messages? What had all this got to do with his mum?

He ran back into the house, grabbed the compass from his bedroom and flipped it open.

What light?

Holding the compass in one hand and his mobile in the other, he looked between them, flinching when the compass started to glow.

He grabbed his coat, ran outside and followed the compass needle, which had turned a rich, deep sea-blue colour and started pulsating. He passed the bakery; the smell of freshly baked bread lingered in the air. Looking down at the compass as he crossed the road, still picturing the text message in his head: "Do you want to know what happened to your mother?"

There was a sudden squeal of brakes and the sound of loud cursing. Almost dropping the compass, he looked up at the driver of a Royal Mail van and whispered an apology. Stepping onto the pavement, head down again, he concentrated on the compass needle. When he reached Currys electrical store he stopped to wipe the moisture off the glass on the compass.

A light flashed in the store window.

He rubbed the glass and peered through. The BBC's morning breakfast programme was showing on all the televisions in the display area.

On one of the televisions to his left, the breakfast programme suddenly faded and the television screen fizzled into a vibrant display of spinning colours. The pattern gradually spread to the other televisions as well. The colours blurred, and bright lights shot out. Then the image of an old man came into focus, and before long, every television in the shop was displaying the same picture.

Who on earth was that?

The old man looked disturbed. His face was wrinkly and wise, worn out like an old leather shoe. His hair was a silvery grey, wiry and messy. Green woollen gloves cut off at the ends, revealing his dirty fingers. His fingernails were black and grimy. He was like some character out of *Oliver Twist*.

Who was this strange man?

One of the television sets suddenly zoomed in on the man's face. He was looking away, as if distracted. He then appeared to reach for something off-screen, but when his hands returned they were empty. He raised his hands in front of his face, then drew the shape of a square in the air. He raised his right forefinger.

'S-n-a-p...' said the man, in a raspy, croaky voice, then pushed his finger down.

Was the old man just playing a game? Tim scratched his head and ruffled his hair. Since his mum had disappeared he had had several sessions with the doctor. They'd put his unusual encounters down to stress: the Guy in the bonfire, the spooky black bird, the strange dreams. But right now he was wide awake. This couldn't be an hallucination, could it? The text message about his mum. That was real. Someone knew something, but who? This old man in the TV?

All the TVs, except for three in the middle of the shop window, were showing static. Eventually, the three TVs in the middle faded into a rainbow of dancing colours once more.

The old man came into focus, this time on the television set in the middle. He was surrounded by spinning colours on the TV sets either side of him.

Tim watched the colours as they twisted and turned. He was reminded of how he used to drip treacle from his spoon and spin it around and around. He would admire the way it ran down the spoon, as if in slow motion.

He looked back at the TV set and stared at the man.

What was the old man thinking? This was *really* happening. This was no dream.

'Who... who are you?' said Tim, his voice shaking. 'What do you know about my mum? The text message. That's from you?'

The old man lifted his right hand and pressed his finger and thumb together. He slid them slowly across his lips from left to right. Why didn't he answer? This couldn't be real.

The TV screen flickered.

Why wasn't there anyone else outside the shop to witness this? Why was he all alone?

'What do you... want?' asked Tim, his voice still shaking. A little perspiration began to trickle down his forehead.

The man winked and reached his hands into the TV sets on either side of him. He seemed to caress the spinning colours as a potter would his clay, before reaching deep into the heart of the colours: the twisted reds; the shades of blue and green; the hints of yellow and purple.

He watched as the old man finished sculpting similarly sized balls of multi-coloured magic in the TVs on either side of him.

The man gripped the balls tightly in his hands, then clenched his fists and seemed to punch right through the TV, towards the shop's window. He unclenched his fists and began rubbing the coloured balls together. His face slowly came out of the TV and he blew on the coloured mass, then, giving it a sharp slap flattened it like a pancake into a multi-coloured disc. Holding the disc with both hands, he pushed towards the glass window. The glass bent around his outstretched arms and pushed out of the window to the street, forcing Tim to step backwards. What was this strange old man making?

The glass around the old man's arms formed a hollow tube, no longer than a loaf of French bread. The tube spun around. He pressed the disc into the end facing Tim and pushed his finger into the other end, making a small hole. He turned to one side, frowning as he looked at the shop's window, then made a sucking motion.

Tim watched as the man sucked a circular section of glass from the shop window, pinched it together with his thumb and forefinger and then placed the resulting glass disc over the hole on the tube. The old man filled his lungs with air from the street, then blew all over the tube as it continued spinning, until the glassy, see-through coating had changed to a frosty colour like compressed snowflakes.

The spinning stopped.

Tim stared at the window. No way! A perfect hole. How was that even possible?

The old man leaned forward, holding out the frosty tube, then squeezed it and presented it to Tim.

Tim stumbled forward to accept the gift, letting it roll gently into his sweaty palms. He clasped the tube tightly, and couldn't help noticing how cold it was on first touch. He looked down at the tube and when he bobbed his head back up the old man had disappeared. He was about to put it to his eye, when he heard a strange sound. He looked straight ahead, through the broken glass, and took a step backwards as the glass window started to repair itself. Just like that, the shop window became whole once more, as if nothing had happened.

Tim rubbed his face several times, his usual early morning wake-up ritual.

Just then, all the televisions reverted to the morning breakfast programme. A weatherman appeared, announcing that there would be light snow across much of the country, and possibly lightning strikes in Cambridge – but only in Cambridge.

Newsflash. The TV weatherman made way for a breaking news report. The presenter of the morning show had tears in his eyes. Thousands of homes destroyed. Thousands of people dead. Water gushing over river banks. Make-shift houses shattered into pieces. Bodies trapped in trees.

Text flashed onto the screen: "worst flood in India's history," it read.

Tim couldn't hear what the presenter was saying, but then he didn't have to: the images said it all. He sighed and rolled the frosty tube in his hand. He was just starting to lift the tube to his eye when he spotted a couple of uniformed children coming towards him. He unzipped his school bag and put the tube inside. As the school children passed he looked in the shop window again. Seeing his reflection, he thought of his mum, then took the compass out of his pocket again.

It wasn't glowing.

"Follow the compass when you see the light," the message had said.

Hedgeton Comprehensive School, Cambridge; 9.00 a.m.

'Homework please...' said Mr Bagley, the maths teacher, as he marched over to his desk.

Some of the class were throwing balls of paper at each other, while others were laughing and joking around. Maybe it was the pre-Christmas spirit – the anticipation of Playstations and iPads. It offered a chance to switch off from the real world for a few hours at a time, a chance to escape the street rioting and looting that had become commonplace in recent times.

Maybe it wasn't the class that was restless, but rather his own state of mind after the encounter with the old man in the shop window. He wondered how he would explain that one to the doctor. His next visit was only a week away. Surely this time he'd believe him. All he needed to do was show him the tube, show him the text message. Surely that would be enough proof that he wasn't going crazy.

'*Homework*, please' shouted Bagley, banging his fist on his desk.

Tim rummaged in his bag to find his homework, but seeing the telescope-like tube, he pulled it out instead. What was it and why had the old man given it to him? Hearing laughter to his right, he glanced towards Michael Tucker. It was obvious that Tucker wasn't going to hand in any homework – just the expression on his face said it all. Tim wondered why Tucker hadn't forced anyone into doing it for him, then he remembered: Tucker just didn't care. Detention had become the norm. Even last year's temporary suspension hadn't taught Tucker a lesson; since his parents had split up, he didn't seem to care about anything anymore – except physical education, that is. It was quite obvious why Tucker liked sport. He liked anything into which he could channel his aggression.

'What you got in the bag, Timbo?' said Michael, looking at the tube in Tim's hand.

Tim ignored the question and swiftly put the tube back in his bag, but Michael was too quick and snatched the bag.

'Hey, give it back!' shouted Tim.

Tim's chair screeched as he shot forwards.

'Now, we wouldn't want any trouble, *would we* Mr Tucker?' said Mr Bagley, looking Michael straight in the eyes. 'I don't think this belongs to you, does it?'

Mr Bagley's words seemed to travel straight up Michael's nasal cavities. He immediately grunted and turned his head away from the teacher. Tim smirked. It was clear that Michael couldn't take it. It didn't get any worse than Bad Breath Bagley. The devilish odours shot right up Michael's nose as his face twisted and contorted. Mr Bagley took the bag from Michael, passed it back to Tim and marched over to his desk. Drawing out each movement,

Michael glanced at his friends, their faces full of sympathy, and slumped down in his chair, defeated.

Tim felt cloudy memories of last night's dream drifting into his head: Tucker grabbing Tim's school bag as he stood in the front garden. He could still picture the looks on Tucker's gang's faces when his front garden had ripped itself from the earth, forcing them to jump off the edge, and started to float through the air with him on it, taking flight high above the streets of Cambridge.

'We're going to start the test in five minutes, boys and girls,' said Mr Bagley. 'I don't want to catch anyone cheating. Remember that you have to choose just three questions from section B. Clear?'

'Yes, Mr Bagley,' said the class.

'And what don't I want to see?'

'Cheating, Mr Bagley.'

'And why's that?'

'Because cheating is for politicians and accountants, Mr Bagley.'

Tim glanced over his side. It was just his luck that Patrick Holmes was sat next to him. The dirtiest boy in the school. If that wasn't bad enough, Patrick was coughing in his face. If the cough were alive and could speak, Tim knew it would say: "I'm going to get you, Timothy Shaw, and I'm going to get you *good*," in a voice like Hannibal Lecter's.

'Papers over. Now... begin,' said Mr Bagley, starting his stopwatch. 'You've got forty five minutes.'

'Achoo,' went Patrick, and greenish-yellow globs of gluey snot shot onto page one of Tim's test paper.

Tim looked at Patrick in disgust, then flipped over the first page of his test paper and pondered on the first question, still struggling to get Patrick out of his mind.

What was wrong with Patrick's face? Patrick let out another tremendous nose fart – so strong it would have been right off the Richter scale. Tim braced himself, then screwed up his face; Patrick was wiping the slimy gunk away with his arm. He was surely going to fail this test. He just couldn't stop thinking about Patrick's snot. Everything about Patrick was a mess; he looked like he had slept in a bucket of hair wax and been put through a car wash.

Ten minutes into the test there was a sudden crack against the classroom window.

'What on earth..?' said Tim, as he looked straight into the eyes of a large, dark bird, perched on the outdoor window sill. The bird's head was scratched like it had been in a fight, and its feathers were faded, like they had been exposed to the sun over a long period of time. There was an unevenness to the bird: it was missing feathers, exposing fleshy lumps on its chubby body. From the corner of its beak, a garden worm's head poked out. The bird turned its head slightly to one side. Slurp. The worm was gone. Then, looking straight at him, the bird bashed its dirty great beak against the window once more.

Crack!

'I'm allergic to birds,' said Patrick. He sneezed again, marking "C" by accident as he did so.

Bang!

'Who said that?' said Mr Bagley, smashing his fist down onto the desk. 'Who's talking?' His bottom lip extended above his top lip: 'who's *cheat-ing*?'

No one answered.

Tim could see a faint scratch on the glass where the bird's beak had struck it. The bird was still staring at him – a soulless stare, reminding Tim of the scariest of places. Its eyes were the colour of egg yolk, with thick black pupils darker than the night. It blinked slowly, sending Tim back to that dream where he was standing on his front garden in mid-air as a large black bird nosedived towards him.

When Bagley wasn't looking, Tim tapped once on the window, just lightly, but the bird didn't flinch. It just continued to sit where it was, motionless. He tapped on the window again, this time more forcefully.

Nothing.

Tim blinked as the bird snapped its neck to the right, then to the left. It looked around most unnaturally, as if it didn't belong to the world at all. As if movement itself were alien.

Tim noticed that instead of circling "A", Patrick had circled "C" by mistake, probably distracted by that creepy bird. He knew Patrick was dirty, but he wasn't stupid.

'Achoo!' went Patrick again, this time spraying his nose glue all over the window. He put his hand to his nose, then wiped it down his trousers.

'You boy!' said Bagley.

Turning and facing Mr Bagley, Tim pointed to himself and asked 'me, Sir?'

'No, not you Shaw. I'm talking to you, Holmes. Stand up lad.'

Tim sighed and turned to the window sill. Patrick stood up.

The bird stretched out its wings, squawked loudly and shrilly, then took flight. A single black feather remained on the window sill. Tim stared at the feather. It blew off the sill and spun around in circles, falling and falling, until it was out of sight.

CHAPTER FOUR

As soon as Tim arrived home, he grabbed a packet of cheese and onion crisps, and a can of Irn Bru from the fridge, and ran upstairs to his bedroom.

He threw his school bag onto the bed and pulled out the telescope-like tube. Lifting one end of the tube to his right eye, he looked through it.

Reds, yellows, greens – and that was just for starters. It was a magical display of animated colours, similar to the images he'd seen on those TV sets earlier that day.

There were no batteries. No obvious mechanisms anywhere.

'It's a kaleidoscope,' muttered Tim as he watched the colours dance, celebrating their new found home. Again, Tim wondered about the old man who gave it to him. What was he supposed to do with it? He couldn't help but be reminded of those fireworks a year earlier and his strange experience with that gunky paint-like substance that had splattered his clothes. The difference was that had just been his imagination. Perhaps when his dad got home he could show him. At least that way he would have someone else to confirm the kaleidoscope's existence before he saw the doctor.

The jiggling colours made him feel weird, like his mind was free. But it was more than just that. He felt a warmth in his chest, like he had just seen a movie with a happy ending. He moved the kaleidoscope away from his eye and the feeling faded.

He put it to his eye again, and pointed it towards his bedroom window.

There it was again: that feeling. A warmth, a confidence.

He glanced over at the compass on his desk and threw the kaleidoscope on top of his bed. It landed on his brilliant white pillow and sank into the material.

Remembering his can of Irn Bru, he pulled back the ring and took a lengthy gulp. He ripped open the crisps, shovelling a handful into his mouth and savouring the taste of the competing flavours.

As he changed out of his school clothes he heard a strange sound – like running water.

It became louder.

He pulled his shirt over his head, and was aware of a bright light suddenly shooting out of his bed. Quickly yanking the shirt off, he focused more closely on the pillow.

'Hey!'

The kaleidoscope. It was melting, quite literally melting over his pillow; a multi-coloured stream of bright, thick, creamy liquid was oozing down his bedsheets, which were now a sea of writhing reds, yellows, pinks and greens.

Tim couldn't help but think of *Joseph and the Amazing Technicolour Dreamcoat*, which he had seen at the theatre. He imagined taking a Bunsen burner to the coat of many colours and watching the colours burn away. That's what he was looking at right now! Kaleidoscope soup dripped down the sides of his bed, forming small glass marbles that danced across the bedroom floor.

Was he losing his mind?

A blue glow over his desk pulled his attention away from the melting colours. He picked up the compass, feeling a dizzy anticipation as it lit up. The needle shook steadily at first. He put his hand on the lid. It felt warm and tingly like before. Tim scratched his head.

Recalling the first text message he had received, he took his mobile out of his school bag and quickly skipped through the messages until he found it again.

"Do you want to know what happened to your mother?"

Did someone really know what happened to his mum? He wanted to scratch his head, but stopped himself. He would soon start losing hair if he kept up the current scratch rate. Tossing the mobile phone onto his bed, he picked up the compass. As he reached the window he pointed the compass towards the street. The needle came to life and started glowing again, pointing north and vibrating, while making a faint humming noise.

He glanced at the photo of his mum on his bedside cabinet, gripped the compass tightly, grabbed his brown leather jacket and left the house.

Tim scooted along Sidney Street, following the compass. He was so engrossed in this that he almost ran into a lamppost. The shops were all closed, and darkness had wrapped itself around their windows and was spreading the cool winter air over them like butter.

A violent cough across the street broke Tim's stride. Who was that man leaning against the shop doorway? He could see the ash at the end of a cigarette glowing as the man sucked in the fumes. In its light, Tim could see the darkness in his eyes. The stranger began strolling along the pavement, the occasional puff of smoke rising into the air.

Tim didn't know why, but this man looked out of place: something about the way he moved, the way he was dressed. The man was probably in his forties, and was wearing a a full length black coat. It looked like leather, but was faintly scaled like fish skin. The cuffs of his white shirt stuck out of the arms of the coat as if the coat was too small. The first three buttons were undone, revealing a wide shirt collar that stuck up proudly. His trousers were thick and a little rumpled. Dark, well-groomed hair was swept back from his forehead. He was staring straight ahead, a vacant look on his face.

As Tim stared at the man, cigarette ash fell onto one of the man's boots. This didn't distract the stranger one bit and he crossed the road, looking down, his cigarette still burning in his mouth. A cyclist swerved around him.

'Why don't you look where you're going?' shouted the cyclist, looking back at the careless pedestrian.

Tim wasn't sure if the man had even noticed the cyclist. Instead the man picked up a newspaper from a nearby newsstand. Before opening it, the man peered over at Tim. Those eyes; something about those eyes just wasn't right.

The man read the front page of the newspaper, then pushed his cigarette through it, making a small, charred hole, through which he proceeded to blow smoke, then looked up at the sky.

Tim followed the man's gaze. A large bird passed overhead and the stranger appeared to smirk.

A radio inside a parked car switched on, startling Tim.

A song was playing on the car radio, and Tim's mind raced back to his dream. It was the creepiest version of "Santa Claus is Coming to Town" Tim had ever heard. It sounded as if the Christmas spirit had been completely sucked out of it.

The man swaggered over to one of the car's passenger doors. He placed both hands on the windowpane, then crouched down and took a good look inside. As Tim watched, the stranger started to rub the glass. Just a few moments later, the windowpane seemed to freeze over and splinter into pieces.

'These things will kill you,' the stranger muttered, turning to face Tim. He dropped his cigarette on the ground and squashed the life out of it. 'Cat got your tongue, boy?'

Tim shrugged. 'What do you want?'

'Nothing you have and everything you desire... Tim-o-thee.'

'Hey, how do you know my...?'

'Name. Ah, yes. I know many things, Tim-o-thee. Things that would make you... wet the bed.'

The man passed the newspaper to Tim.

"Rival Oxford gangs in street murder, five killed," the front page headline read.

'A terrible, terrible thing,' said the man, shaking his head. 'And they were so. Well, delicious. Oh, but where are my manners? The name's Daniel.'

'Delicious?' said Tim.

Daniel smirked and pulled his hand away sharply.

'What do you want?' asked Tim, screwing up the newspaper and throwing it into the rubbish bin by the newsstand.

Daniel reached into his deep pockets and pulled out a photo frame. He stroked the frame as a child would stroke their dog.

'Oh mummy-mummy... please don't leave me. Don't go. Don't leave me and dad-dy all alone...'

Tim flinched as Daniel turned the photo around.

It was his mum. The same photo he kept by his bedside.

'Hey, where did you get that?' said Tim.

Tim lunged forwards to grab the photo, but Daniel lifted it above his head. Tim pushed Daniel, making him lose his balance. The photo flew into the air and landed on Daniel's stomach just as he hit the ground.

'Nice move,' said Daniel, jumping back on his feet and putting the photo back inside his coat.

'What do you know about my mum? What have you done to her?'

'Your mum is *dead.* Dead as a door nail.'

Tim struck out, catching Daniel's shoulder. 'You're lying.'

'Isn't that what the police said? Missing presumed dead?'

Tim didn't want to believe it. He felt his legs weaken. It was true, the police had told them to assume the worst. There had been no ransom note, no sign of a struggle.

'I'm not leaving until you tell me what you've done to her, you creep,' said Tim.

'That's the spirit. Quite the gutsy one aren't you? I'm sensing a change in you, Tim-o-thee.'

'Get lost,' said Tim.

Daniel approached him, put his hand on his shoulder and reached for his neck. He breathed in deeply, absorbing Tim's scent. 'Yes, a real change. I hadn't noticed before.'

'Before?'

'You think this is the first time we've met?'

'I don't know what you're talking about,' said Tim. 'I don't *know* you.'

'Your mum. Now she was *real* special. I had no idea it ran in the family.'

'Where is she!' said Tim, clenching his fists.

Daniel shrugged.

'Feeling any....different?' he asked, sniffing more loudly. 'I sense danger in you.'

'Just tell me what you've done to her!'

'Temper, temper. My frightened *little* boy.'

'I'm not frightened.'

Daniel lifted his head up and breathed in deeply, fixing a stare on Tim. He raised his hands above his head and let out a deep, throaty laugh.

Tim looked on as Daniel's dirty finger nails extended – extended into claws. Daniel's eyes darkened until they were as black as coal.

'What kind of *monster* are you?' asked Tim, stepping backwards.

Daniel curled his fingers together, drew them close to his mouth and whispered, 'this is the part where you run...'

Tim glanced from side to side, then began sprinting down the street. A screech came from behind him, and Tim looked over his shoulder. What the hell?

A huge bird was swooping towards him, wings outstretched. Tim couldn't remember seeing anything like it. It was no blackbird – it was no ordinary bird at all. The underside of its wings had purplish veins that pulsated as it gained speed. Its claws were stretched out towards him.

Tim's pace quickened, and he raced towards the Grand Arcade shopping centre on his left. The surprised faces of passers-by flashed in front of him. The bird tore at his jacket, scratching the leather with its claws. It couldn't end like this. He had to find somewhere. Somewhere the bird couldn't go.

The shops were becoming a blur, but he noticed a bank on the opposite side of the street. It had a sliding door. There was no way the bird could fly through glass. He crossed the street, looking over his shoulder as he went. The bird was catching up with him again.

When he reached the door it slid open, but then closed abruptly, and the bird smashed into the glass, scratching it with its beak. Tim looked out of the window and the bird dropped to the ground and lay there, motionless.

An old woman, who was taking cash out of one of the ATMs, looked at Tim then at the bird. Tim sprinted out of the building and turned to his right, looking over his shoulder every few metres until he got to Christ Lane, where he made another right. He didn't stop running until he reached the bus station.

Short of breath, he looked towards the tree-lined park by the station, then at a bus that just pulled in. What was that bird-thing? He bent over and clasped his hands around his knees, coughing as fumes from the bus flooded his lungs. Just what was his mum involved in?

That night Tim couldn't sleep. Why did people have to die? How would it *feel* to be dead? The very thought of not existing one day just made his brain hurt.

Could it be that one day he would just tire of living and *want* to die? And where did people go after they died? Why was it that he couldn't stop thinking about death, while all his friends could think about was about how cool it was to pull wings off house flies?

Of course, he knew what the reason was: they had never found his mum. Was she really dead, as this stranger, Daniel, had said?

He lay in bed for hours trying to imagine the blackness and emptiness that must follow death. The very thought of his consciousness not being there anymore just baffled him. What would happen to his thoughts? His ideas? His dreams? If only his mum could have said goodbye, given him some closure. It was the police who had told him to assume the worst.

As his mind tumbled further into darkness, images of the smoking man in the long black coat filled his head: the claws, the haunting voice and those menacing eyes.

'Cat got your tongue, boy?'

He pictured the bird that had smashed into his classroom window. It looked just like the bird Daniel had changed into. Was that what Daniel had meant when he said it wasn't the first time they had met? What did this bird-like creature – this monster – want from him?

One thing was for sure. *Someone* knew what happened to his mum and *someone* was trying to help him find the truth. Whoever had sent the compass, the text messages.

He rubbed his eyes. Stretching to the end of his bed, he peered through the curtain. He couldn't remember ever seeing such a black night. A night without stars. A night without hope.

CHAPTER FIVE

Hedgeton Comprehensive School, Friday.
Tim's compass hadn't glowed all day. He'd
found it hard to concentrate in school. Memories of
his mum. The hurt and pain of the last year. The
sound of that bird ripping at his jacket.

As he strolled into art club, sixth former Gemma
Bowen stood in front of the class.

'Evening all,' said Gemma, arching her legs and
tugging the lapels of her Edwardian looking creamy
blouse. 'Glad you could make it. You might be ugly,
but at least you're on time!'

Tim laughed.

'Today,' she seemed to lose her next words,' ...to-
day, we're going to do something a little different.'

Tim smiled, 'don't we always..'

Gemma acknowledged Tim with a winning smile, her stunning green eyes practically sparkling.

'What I'd like you all to do today is explore one of your dreams. Interpret it. Try to capture the very essence of its meaning. Think of it in two dimensions. What it tells you on surface and what it *really* means.'

Tim felt his stomach turn. There was no escape from dreams lately. Was she in on this to?

'Who can tell me which artist was greatly inspired by dream analysis in their work?' she said.

Tim raised his hand first.

'Yes, Tim?'

'Dali.'

'That's right, Tim. Salvador Dali was influenced by Freud. But not only Freud. If you look at one of his most famous pieces, "The Persistence of Memory", he was also inspired by Einstein's theories. The relative nature of time itself.'

Tim turned to admire a large poster of "The Persistence of Memory" as Gemma unrolled it and stuck it on the wall behind her.

'Four clocks melting in an empty desert,' said one of the class.

'That's right, four clocks. But does anyone know why the clocks are melting?'

'Probably it means that time has lost its relevance in dreams,' said Tim, '..like time itself is distorted.'

'That's one interpretation. It could also suggest that the melting clocks represent our memories. How our memories themselves can be vague. Or short lived. So in the title of the painting, Dali is demonstrating a degree of humour.'

'Do you think all art can be explained, you know, like this?' said Chloe, the youngest member of the class.

'Yes, Chloe, I think so. I think there's a rational explanation for everything,' said Gemma.

Tim frowned, thinking of all those police interviews. The media coverage. The false hope. Where was the logic explaining his mum's disappearance?

'Even for....well...aliens, life on mars....monsters?' said Chloe.

Gemma smiled. 'Well, Chloe. I think if there were aliens....monsters, we'd probably have found them by now. Don't you? No, Chloe. I think the only logical explanation is that there are no aliens. There are no such things as monsters. Not real monsters anyway. That's why our imagination is so important. That's why art is so important. It lets us explore the impossible. It lets us ask, "what if?"'

Tim wasn't sure what it was about Gemma he liked the most. Yes, he'd a soft spot for brunettes. But it went beyond that. She wasn't ashamed of her passion for drinking cold chocolate milk, even in school. She was only a couple of years older than him and ever so witty, but with a kind of eccentricity that made her unpredictable. Maybe that's what he admired the most. The uncertainty. It wasn't her height, that's for sure, as she was at least another three inches taller than him.

No one could deny, Gemma Bowen brought art to life and she brought it to life with an infectious passion – even if she did sometimes sound older than her years.

'What I'd like you to show me, is how *you* interpret your own dreams.'

Tim heard Gemma move through the classroom, passing comments as she went from one student to another. Tim liked Gemma's voice. It was crisp, clear and very sure of itself. She'd the authority of a teacher, but was very cool with it.

'That's awesome, Jo,' said Gemma as she admired Jo Borril's journey into Gothic castles and vampires.

Tim looked down at his canvas. The brush sure felt good in his hand. His brush strokes glided over the canvas with artistic precision and created the most unusual shapes and bursts of colour. This was Tim's dream all right. It was still vivid in his memory.

'Hmm...that's curious, Tim,' said Gemma, peering over his shoulder.

Tim continued to steer his brush with confidence, encouraged that Gemma's curiosity had been tickled.

He almost seemed to glow as he painted. It was as if his brush was a natural extension of his body.

Gemma had often complimented him on his creative flare.

When he finished, he stood back from his painting and sighed, running his hand over his face – up and down, several times. He remembered the moment in his dream when the garden picked up speed, forcing him to lose his balance and almost fall off. Passing an old tramp like figure - dressed like he came from another century.

'That's really awesome,' said Gemma, drawing a pencil away from her lips and pointing it at Tim's painting.

'It makes me feel like.... like...,' said Chloe.

'Like you're on top of the world,' her friend interrupted.

'I feel....funny..,' remarked another.

What had happened to them all? It was like they'd all been drinking some kind of happy soup.

'And what's that supposed to be?' said Gemma, as she pointed to the left side of the painting, her eyes sparkling brighter.

'Is that a fountain?' said Chloe '...with speakers sticking out of it?'

'Er...well, yes...,' said Tim.

A boy at the back of the class, who Tim couldn't quite place, suddenly burst into song. He looked at Tim with a straight face - dark tints below his eyes as if he were wearing some kind of Gothic eye liner. He bellowed out the first lines from Queen's Bohemian

Rhapsody and pushed back on his chair, forcing the chair to squeal as it catapulted backwards.

Tim's mind flashed back to his dream once more...as two speakers shot out of the fountain in his garden to the same Queen ditty. Just who *was* this Goth Boy? How could he know about *that* song?

Goth Boy stood up and strode over to him, turning his head to one side with a crack as he fixed his stare on Tim's painting.

The boy flinched and looked like he was going to vomit, turning his gaze quickly away from the painting. He gave Tim an evil look and stomped across the classroom, a blank expression on his face. But those eyes. Green. Intense.

Who was this guy? Tim struggled to remember his name. Come to that, he struggled to remember ever seeing him in the class before.

Goth Boy marched over to the classroom door, stomped out and slammed it shut.

'Who *was* that?' said Tim.

Gemma looked puzzled, 'I....I don't quite remember his name.'

'Me neither,' said Tim, as other classmates nodded.

Tim dashed over to where Goth Boy had been sitting and twisted the canvas around. He raised his eyebrows.

Right there on the canvas was the clear image of Tim stood on his front garden. He was being attacked by a bird.

All Tim could see were the bird's claws. The sound of Daniel's voice.

"Your mum is dead. Dead as a door nail."

'That's just sick,' said Chloe, as she turned her head away from the painting, '..the birds..they're pecking your eyes out...yuck.'

'He's seriously disturbed,' said Gail.

'You're all *so* conventional,' said Jo. 'Art's not all about sunflowers and melting clocks you know.'

'Wait a minute. He's *not* in our club,' said Gemma, '...who is he?' She looked around the classroom for a reaction. Everyone looked at each other.

Tim went in pursuit, opened the classroom door and peered down both ends of the corridor.

Empty.

Returning to the classroom, Tim looked at Goth Boy's painting again. How could anyone possibly know about his dream? Tim hadn't mentioned it to a living soul.

But there was an inconsistency there. The bird never pecked his eyes out. At least not in *his* dream. The thought of those birds feasting on his eyeballs made him want to vomit and he felt a sickly warm liquid rise up his throat.

'God, I'm gonna be sick.'

He clasped his hand to his mouth and sucked in a pocket of air to fight it off.

Why would someone paint something so terrible? Why his eyes?

He glanced over at his watch. While no one was looking, he flipped open the compass under his desk.

He squinted as the blue glow almost blinded him and closed the lid shut.

He had to continue the search. But the search for what?

The truth about his mum's disappearance? A body in a grave?

Tim felt his nerves tighten and his throat dry. He pocketed the compass and marched out of the art room.

⚔

Outside the school he flipped open the compass and realised he was going in the wrong direction.

Tim noticed the glow around the compass was getting brighter. The needle twitched when he reached the entrance of a nearby park. He looked around, but all he could see were park benches, swings and lots of trees. Right in front of him was the largest of the trees. A fine oak tree that probably dated back at least a hundred years, if not more.

One large, black bird was perched on a branch, high up on the tree. Tim shivered as it took flight, passing over his head, forcing him to picture his eyes being gouged out in Goth Boy's painting.

He approached a pub that overlooked the park. It was still early in the evening, but the music coming out of the pub boomed into the stratosphere. A few winter revellers were standing outside, beer glasses in hands, chatting, joking. Young couples sucking each other's lips off, like they were draining the life out of each other.

Tim slipped the compass into his coat pocket as one of the revellers moved away from the crowd towards him.

'Can I get you one, Tim?' he said.

'Hey, you're...,' said Tim.

'Yes...I'm the guy from your art club. Sorry about that. It was just a bit of fun. Let me get you a beer.'

How could Goth Boy pass for eighteen? He was clearly younger. No facial hair, boyish face. Though maybe his weirdness made him pass for older – or perhaps it was that whole Goth look, the eye liner - those intense green eyes that looked straight through you.

'No, thanks,' said Tim, shaking his head.

Goth Boy turned to Tim, took a big gulp of beer, swallowing until he finished his glass and whispered, 'go on...have a beer...beer good. Beer *very* good,' his face turning sour.

Tim heard a car accelerate down the street. Rap music blasted out, as the youths inside shouted obscenities at the small crowd outside the pub. He glanced at the car. The driver braked and cruised slowly along the curb. One of the men in the front passenger seat opened his window, held out a bag, shook it....and looked at Tim.

'You buying?' said the man in the passenger seat.

Tim moved aside as Goth Boy brushed past him, fists clenched.

'He's just a kid,' said Goth Boy. 'He doesn't want your drugs, but I'll take them off your hands for free,' he said, grabbing the bag and twisting the man's wrist into a lock.

The car brakes screeched and Tim smelt burning rubber. The driver and two big guys on the back seat got out the car and surrounded him.

The driver wore a blue tracksuit with the hood down. His head partially shaved, with small tattoos on his neck. But it was his head that scared Tim the most. His face looked like the surface of the moon, with sunken skin for craters. Was it a bad case of acne? He was Mr Crater Face all right.

Tim felt a blow to his stomach as Crater Face punched him. As he tumbled to the ground he saw Crater Face push Goth Boy against the car and snatch the bag back.

'You better pick on someone your own size,' said Crater Face and forced Goth Boy to release his lock on the passenger's wrist.

Tim stood up and heard Goth Boy take a deep breath as he turned his head to each of the three men.

'Shhhhh...,' said Goth Boy, as he grabbed the bag back, pressing his forefinger to his mouth.

Tim turned to the men outside the car. They looked confused and uneasy. It was as if they couldn't move. Paralysed from the waist down. Like Goth Boy had cast a spell on them. The man in the passenger seat slammed the car door open, rammed it against Goth Boy's legs and forced him to the ground.

Tim felt an arm wrap around his throat as Crater Face lunged forward. He couldn't move.

'Now *that's* what I call a head lock,' said Crater Face in a hoarse voice.

Goth Boy was back on his feet. He brushed off some of the small pebbles that had stuck to his trousers and turned to Crater Face, clasping one of the pebbles in his hand. He looked at the pebble, then at Crater Face and proceeded to place it delicately on his tongue. He retracted his tongue as a lizard would eat a fly. As he swallowed the pebble, he gulped loudly and licked his lips.

'Oh, now I am *real* scared Pebble-boy,' said Crater Face.

The Goth whispered, 'Let....him....go,' and paused. He waited no more than a couple of seconds.

'Let.. him.. go......*now!*' said Goth Boy.

Crater Face laughed. 'You don't scare me,' he said.

Tim struggled from Crater Face's grip.

The Goth turned to look at the other three men.

'What the...?' said Crater Face, staring at his paralysed associates.

'Your friends? Now *they* look scared,' said Goth Boy, glancing at Crater Face's friends, before sending a swift nod to Tim.

Tim stamped his foot hard on Crater Face's foot. The arm around his neck loosened and he bolted down the street as fast as he could.

He wanted to ask Goth Boy about the painting. He wanted to know how he could possibly know about the dream. But right now he had to get away.

Tim kept running until he reached the bingo hall and hid inside. He peered around the door to see if he was being followed.

Who was this guy from his art club? Why was he helping?

He opened the compass again, its blue glow lighting the entrance of the doorway.

The glow stopped.

He sighed and flipped the compass shut.

'That's enough trouble for one night,' he said, and started the long walk home.

CHAPTER SIX

Gemma Bowen finished up in the art room. She collected all the paintings that had dried and put them in a large leather art folder. She shivered as a vision of Goth Boy's expressionless face entered her mind. How could she not have noticed him in the room? Who was he? Why had his painting freaked out Tim so much? She had too many questions on her mind as she cycled home that evening.

══╬ ╬══

After a disastrous Spaghetti Bolognese, Gemma opened the art folder and took out the first batch of paintings. It was time to grade them. Better to do it

Friday night and keep the weekend free, especially as she had the house to herself this weekend.

She pondered for a moment. Was this really any way for an attractive teenager to spend her Friday night?

That was until she glanced over at Tim's painting...then the thought melted away...her motivation restored. A warmth. A comforting embrace.

What was it about *that* painting?

Smash. Clatter.

Was it coming from the kitchen?

Gemma lost her balance. 'What the...?'

She dropped the paintings onto the dining table and watched helplessly as they slid off the edge and flew across the room towards the sofa.

Tim's painting was the last to land and floated over a well-lit floor lamp by the sofa, sticking to its side.

She rushed out of the living room and scooted into the kitchen.

'Marmalade,' she said, observing broken glass all over the floor. Sticky marmalade jam was splattered everywhere, surrounded by smashed crockery.

'Einstein!' she shouted, 'look what you've done!'

The marmalade wasn't alone. Lapping it up, was Einstein, her treasured cat.

Einstein stopped licking the marmalade and ran out of the kitchen.

She turned to Einstein's bowl. The bowl with "E=mc^2" etched into it, in a childlike black font on a purple background. 'And you haven't even touched *your* food!'

Gemma reached for the dustpan and cleaned up the mess, cursing Einstein as she scooped up the debris, bagged it and dumped it in the pedal bin.

'Oh god. Is that general waste, or...doesn't glass have to be...' She couldn't be doing with all this environmentally friendly malarkey.

Back in the living room she looked at the paintings scattered all over the floor. 'Now...where was I?'

She picked them up and put them back on the dining table.

'What are you looking at, Einstein, you little monster,' she said, following Einstein's head as he looked up at the ceiling. 'Oh my god, what on earth? Do you see what I see, Einstein?' She stood back, eyebrows raised, as she gaped at the pattern on her ceiling.

Einstein was silent for a moment before he let out a soft meow and darted out of the room. From the front window Gemma watched him run up the street.

Stupid cat.

She looked up at her living room ceiling again. 'That's just impossible.'

Somehow, some way, the floor lamp was projecting an image from Tim's painting onto her living room ceiling. Except it wasn't Tim's painting anymore. Not exactly, anyway. It was missing some details. Some colours.

She fumbled through the art club register for Tim's contact number and reached for her mobile. Her finger hovered over the buttons before springing into action.

'Come on, come on...pick up, pick up.'

CHAPTER SEVEN

'Hello?' said Tim.

'Tim? Tim is that you?'

'Who's that?'

'It's Gemma. Gemma from art club.'

'What is it? What do you want?'

'You have to get over here right away. And I mean right now!'

'Why, what's happened?' said Tim.

'You have to see it. Just get over here and you'll see. Look, I'll text you my address. Just get here as quickly as you can. You have to see this.'

'Okay, okay, calm down – I'll come over now.'

Tim took the bus to Gemma's house, which was conveniently on the same street as one of his friends.

'So, what's all the f...?' Before Tim could finish, Gemma pulled him by the arm into the dining area.

'Look!' she said, pointing up at the ceiling.

'What is it?'

'Can't you see what it is?'

'Well..,' he paused, '..some kind of maze? A map?'

'Wait,' said Gemma, as she marched over to the living area.

'What are you doing?' said Tim.

'Just wait, you'll see,' said Gemma, as she lifted the painting off the floor lamp and skipped back to the dining table, thrusting it in front of Tim.

'See..,' she said, pushing the other paintings aside.

Tim looked at the painting. 'But that's....'

'Exactly,' said Gemma, '...that's not the picture on my ceiling.'

Tim picked up the painting and held it up. 'No...I mean, it's *my* painting!'

He knelt down by the floor lamp and held his painting over the light.

There it was again.

A map.

'Mint!' said Tim, waving his hand between the light and his painting.

'Come on, Tim,' she said. 'This is serious. Doesn't this just freak you out? Just a little?'

Tim's mouth was wide open. 'Quick, where's your camera?' he said.

'Just a minute,' said Gemma, as she skipped over to the dresser next to the dining table and scooped her hands through the drawers. 'Here, take it.'

Tim twisted a few settings and snapped a picture of the map on the ceiling.

'USB Cable..,' he snapped.

Gemma pulled out a white cable from the drawer and passed it to Tim. 'Now what?'

'Your computer, where is it?'

'Upstairs, why?'

'Lead the way, come on Gemma, this is important.'

'What do you mean it's important. What are you talking about?'

'I don't have time to explain now Gemma, and you wouldn't believe me if I told you. But I think this map. I think it's important. I think it's got something to do with Mum.'

Gemma shrugged. 'Your mum? But your mum, she's....I mean, she's missing.'

'Exactly. She's missing and you've got a map on your ceiling.'

'But Tim, you surely don't think..'

'I don't think it's a coincidence. If you'd seen what I've seen these last twenty four hours, you'd believe pretty much anything, I can tell you.'

'Well, I think you're ever so slightly mad, but come on...follow me.'

Tim followed her upstairs. Once in her den, he noticed her computer. Of course, it had to be an Apple Mac didn't it. These arty types.

'What are you going to do?' asked Gemma.

Tim uploaded the image to her computer and started dragging windows across the screen.

'I'm going to find where it is,' he said, as he started to match the image against a database of maps.

'I need. I need...,' said Tim.

'What?' said Gemma.

Tim looked up. 'Tea!'

'Oh, and I suppose you want me to...,' said Gemma.

Tim nodded, 'oh yes, that would be great.'

Gemma sighed as she made her way downstairs to the kitchen

'Earl grey! And don't forget the milk,' shouted Tim.

'Yuck! You're one of *those...*'

When she returned, tea in one hand, cold chocolate milk in the other, Tim clasped his hands around the mug.

'Right. We'll leave that running overnight, and we should get some idea in the morning,' he said.

'You're joking aren't you? Overnight? I thought computers were supposed to be fast.'

She paused.

'Some idea of what?' she said.

'Like I said, where it is. If it's a real map. If it's a real place, we'll find it.'

Tim looked at the complex images on the monitor as they flicked through hundreds of maps in seconds, looking for a match.

'But it's from your painting, Tim. It can't be a real place. That's impossible.'

'This map. It seems to be in two parts,' said Tim, as he looked at the main map image on the screen. 'This part,' he said, pointing at the image on the left, 'seems to be a specific building.....and this part is probably a room.'

Gemma nodded. 'But Tim, why do you think this has anything to do with your mum?'

Tim reached for his mobile and showed Gemma the message:

"Do you want to know what happened to your mother?"

'You don't think someone's just playing a sick joke on you? Tucker?'

'No, Gemma. Definitely not,' he said, flipping to the next message:

"Follow the compass when you see the light."

Gemma shrugged. 'That's very cryptic. What does it mean?'

'It's about a compass I got in the post yesterday.'

'A compass? For real? And you really think this is about your mum?'

'Of course. Ever since this all started I've been chased by a man who can change into a bird, I've been given a kaleidoscope from a man inside a TV set, and I had a run in with some drug dealers. It's just crazy, Gemma. And now this. A map on your ceiling. It has to mean something.'

'It sounds like you're getting mixed up between fantasy and reality, Tim. You're just confusing your dream with the real world.'

'No, I'm not,' said Tim. 'You saw the map yourself. It's not magic is it? Can you explain it?'

'Well, no, I can't explain it, but there has to be a rational explanation, Tim. A man who can change into a bird? Wasn't there a bird in that boy's painting in art club?'

'Yes, that's right, there was.'

'Well there you are then, you probably had a nightmare last night.'

'No, it's not like that, I'm telling you, it's all real.'

'Tim, people don't turn into birds. There's no such thing as monsters. Surely you know that?'

'I wouldn't believe it myself if I hadn't seen it with my own eyes, Gemma.'

'If you're right about this map,' said Gemma, 'come back in the morning and we'll see where it is. But you better go and get some rest, Tim. I think the stress of this last year is getting to you. It's completely understandable.'

Tim sighed and followed Gemma downstairs – leaving her house feeling low. How could he prove to her that this was all real?

CHAPTER EIGHT

When Tim reached Gemma's house the next morning, his sensitive nose was hit by a delicious wave of smells...freshly brewed tea, pancakes and if he wasn't mistaken, cinnamon rolls.

'Morning,' said Tim. 'How are those pancakes coming along?'

Gemma smiled and scooped the pancakes out of the frying pan onto two large white plates, placing the plates on the breakfast bar. A small pot of tea was already waiting for Tim.

'Is it...?' said Tim.

'Yes....it's Earl Grey. Of *course*,' she said.

'You don't live alone here, do you?'

'Of course not. My parents are away for the weekend.'

'Lucky you.'

After breakfast Tim was keen to resume the mystery of the projected map on Gemma's ceiling and ran upstairs, Gemma tailing behind.

'It's 92% complete,' said Tim, sipping his tea.

'Can't you make this thing go any faster?' said Gemma, as she drummed her fingers on the corner of the desk.

'Well, I think it's nearly there.'

'What do you think this second part is? You said last night you thought it might be a room?' said Gemma.

'Maybe, maybe not,' he said.

'Hey, what if this map leads us to Hogwarts?'

'Funny, Gemma. You're *so* funny.'

'Well you have to admit, this is pretty strange. Unless you're just playing a big joke on me?'

'The only way I'm going to panic,' said Tim, 'is if the computer comes back and says "*Computer says no.*"'

The computer beeped.

'Hey, it's finished!' he said, a clear octave higher.

Gemma peered at the screen.

'Well, the computer definitely doesn't say no,' he said, pointing at the screen. 'Computer says "Trinity College, Cambridge." Hey. That's right here.'

'You're telling me that your painting has a map of Trinity College hidden inside it? That's just crazy.'

'Hey, computers don't lie,' he said. 'Look. It's there in black and white.'

'So, what now?'

'We go to Trinity College, of course. We have to find out what this is all about. Where it leads.'

'But we've got no idea what we'll find in the college, Tim. It might not mean anything.'

Tim sighed. 'We know this map's in two parts. Trinity College. That's part one. Part two must be one of the rooms.'

'Let's print it out and get going then,' she said, 'it's not like I've got anything better to do today. If nothing else, I want to say I told you so when you see there are no such things as monsters, or men coming out of TV screens.'

'I know you don't believe me, Gemma. You didn't give me chance to explain last night. Just look at this,' said Tim, passing Gemma the compass.

'So the compass, it's real?'

'You can see for yourself.'

Gemma pressed the button and opened the compass. 'Nice piece of work. It's your dad's?'

'No, Gemma, I told you last night; it came in the post on Thursday.'

'So who sent it then?'

'I don't know. There wasn't a note.'

'What about the text message. The one about following the compass when it lights up?'

'That's what I wanted to tell you last night. It did light up. I mean, it glowed and I followed it to the electrical store. That's where I got the kaleidoscope.'

'You mentioned that yesterday,' she said. 'So the compass, you said it lights up. But look, it's not doing anything.'

'I can see that. I don't know how it works. It was like that during school for most of yesterday. It was only after art club that it started to glow.'

'You can see how all this sounds, can't you?'

Tim shrugged. 'I'm just asking you to believe me, Gemma. You remember the boy in art club, the Goth? Even you couldn't remember seeing him before. He knew something about my dream, I'm telling you Gemma, I haven't told anyone about my dream. How could he know about it. You heard him singing. That was the same song in my dream. It's impossible, he can't know what I'm dreaming about.'

'I don't know, maybe he picked up something from your painting.'

'No way. But it's even weirder. Last night, before you called me, he helped me to get away from these thugs selling drugs. So why would he help me?'

'You're right, that doesn't make much sense. Unless you dreamed it.'

Tim turned to the image of the map on the computer. 'Let's just print it out and get going. You'll see I'm right about all of this.'

'I know how important it is for you to understand what happened to your mum. I'll come with you, of course. I'm worried about you though. I think your dreams are confusing you.'

Tim shook his head, printed out the map and within minutes they were on their way.

Arriving in the centre of town, Tim followed Gemma on the short walk to Trinity College. Everyday life continued around him as if nothing unusual had happened or was ever likely to happen. Postmen were on their rounds, dodging barking dogs and flinching as killer letterboxes from hell tried to bite their fingers off. Old age pensioners reminisced about times gone by, reminding their grandchildren not to get old.

As they approached Trinity Street, Tim stopped and went pale.

'What's wrong with you?' said Gemma.

'Look,' said Tim, pointing to a man outside a shop. 'It's him.'

'Who?' asked Gemma.

'Daniel. He tried to get me last night. He knows something about my mum,' he gestured for Gemma to come closer and whispered, 'he's not human. He's the one I told you about. The one that turned into a bird.'

'Come on, Tim...'

'No, Gemma. I know it sounds crazy. Last night he told me Mum was dead and he came after me. He changed into a bird. I saw it happen, Gemma. His hands turned into claws. His eyes went all black.'

'I think that Goth's painting is getting to you.'

'You think it's anymore crazy than what happened in your living room?'

'Well, there has to be a logical explanation for that. I told you.'

'Come on Gemma, just what kind of logic is there for a map hidden inside a painting. Unless you think I did it on purpose?'

Gemma shrugged. 'He's going into that coffee shop, look. Shall we follow him?'

'I'm not sure about that. Who knows what he'll do if he sees me. Shouldn't we just go to the college?'

'We will. But let's see what he's up to. Where's your sense of adventure? If you really think he knows what happened to your mum, maybe we can find something out.'

'You might be right. It's a public place. Hopefully he's not stupid enough to try anything there.' Tim grabbed Gemma's arm. 'But you go in first, okay. I'll walk behind you. I don't want him to see me.'

As Tim bowed his head and followed Gemma inside he was hit by the strong smell of coffee and freshly baked cookies. The place was bustling.

'Let's sit there, by the window,' said Tim.

Tim sat on a table sandwiched between Daniel's and a small group of teenagers. He covered his face with his hand and crouched in his seat.

'What's he doing?' said Tim.

'He's ordering an espresso,' whispered Gemma.

'I'll bring your coffee over when it's ready,' said the waitress looking at Daniel, 'and what name is it?'

'Daniel, they call me Daniel.'

'What time is it?' asked one of the teenagers on the table next to Tim.

'It's nearly quarter two,' replied another.

'Hey, I've got to be at work in fifteen minutes.'

A couple of the others in the group nodded. 'Me too,' they said.

'Come on, let's go,' said the ringleader, as he pulled his chair back.

The waitress brushed past Tim and passed an espresso to Daniel as the ringleader stood up.

Tim looked over his shoulder as Daniel turned to the young group of teenagers.

'No work. Not today,' said Daniel, as he exhaled smoke from his mouth and covered their faces. When the smoke cleared, their faces looked confused.

'Another coffee?' the ringleader asked the others, sitting back down in his chair.

'Did you see that?' whispered Tim. 'Whatever he said, it's made them forget about their jobs. You heard, they were about to leave..'

'Yes, that's weird,' said Gemma, 'where did that smoke come from?'

Tim shrugged. 'I told you. He's not human.'

'Come on Tim, don't start all that again.'

Tim watched Daniel as he smiled and winked at the waitress, swallowed his espresso and left the coffee shop.

Tim turned to the coffee shop window. Daniel hovered outside the door.

'I can't see him now. What's he doing?' said Gemma.

'He's taking a pack of smokes from his pocket,' said Tim. 'It's like he's just staring at the packet. Something's making him smile.'

Tim could just make out the words on the packet as Daniel flipped the packet round.

"SMOKING KILLS."

'He's flicking his thumb..,' said Tim. 'Why is he...?'

Tim raised his eyebrows. 'Hey! He's just made a flame with his thumb. He's lighting a smoke now.'

'Tim?'

'What?'

'Look over here.'

'Why, what is it?'

'There's someone else sitting on Daniel's table now.'

Tim turned to look. 'Him!'

'You know him?'

'It's the postman. The one who delivered the compass.'

Tim turned to the window. 'Look away, look away, he's coming back in.' He covered his face again and pulled the compass out of his pocket. He passed the compass to Gemma and watched her spin it around on her palm.

'Eight sides?' she said.

Tim took the compass back and shook it lightly. 'Come on, come on...,' he said. 'I'm sure it's trying to take me somewhere. You saw the text messages I showed you.'

'Who sent the texts?'

'I don't know, the number was blocked.'

'You think it was him?' said Gemma, glancing at the postman.

'I don't know. If he's with Daniel, maybe they're in it together.'

'If this postman is really in it with Daniel, I don't think he would send you a text message. That doesn't make sense. It sounds more like whoever sent you the text messages is trying to help you. And whoever sent the text messages, sent you the compass.'

'Maybe they're both sick. He must be in on it. Why else would he be here...with him?'

Gemma shrugged. 'Shhh...let's listen to what their saying and maybe we'll find out.'

CHAPTER NINE

'When are you going to give it up?' said Daniel. The postman shrugged, 'When you and your kind retire, *Deceiver*.'

Daniel smirked, pulled a board from his inside coat pocket and opened it up. Once on the table, chess pieces rose up out of the empty squares, filling both sides with ornate black and white chess pieces.

'Colour?' said Daniel.

The postman said nothing and turned the board around.

Daniel smirked. 'Black. That's a little predictable, don't you think?'

Turning to the bookcase by his side, Daniel picked up a book. He placed his palm over the cover, opened it, slammed the book onto the table and spun the book around to face the postman, just as the postman moved his first chess piece.

'History...my friend, is going to rewrite itself,' said Daniel, as the words on the page appeared to shiver and shake.

'And you know...you know they just aren't going to understand. I mean, *really* understand,' said Daniel.

The postman signalled to the waitress.

'Espresso for him,' said the postman.

'And a tall latte for my *friend* here,' said Daniel, with a wink to the waitress.

Reaching for his pack of cigarettes, Daniel pulled out his thumb and forefinger, flicked his thumb upwards and lit his cigarette.

The waitress turned to Daniel. 'Sorry, sir. No smoking indoors.'

'I think you're mistaken, Miss,' said Daniel, pointing to the smoking sign on the door, after the red circle around the cigarette went from red to green and the thick black line through the cigarette disappeared.

'That doesn't make sense,' said the waitress. 'I've never seen *that* sign before.'

As the game of chess played out like a Saturday afternoon game of tennis, Daniel was distracted by an elderly woman two tables away.

'Ah...is the smoke *upsetting* you?' said Daniel.

The old woman coughed, held her hand to her mouth and nodded.

He moved his espresso cup to the edge of the table and sank his cigarette in the cup. It sizzled and floated to the top.

'You didn't have to...,' said the woman.

Daniel held his hand up. 'No matter,' he said. 'Let me *help* you.'

He pulled out his chair and swaggered over to the old woman. He looked her up and down. She must have been at least seventy, dressed in a thick blue flowery dress that looked like it had enjoyed re-birth after a former life as a pair of curtains.

He held out his hand and helped the woman to her feet. She stared at her walking stick, leant against the bookcase. Her face distressed.

'Finished your *tea*? Your deli-*cious*, tasty tea?' said Daniel. 'It is *tasty* isn't it? I mean, my smoking hasn't disturbed the flavour in any way, has it?'

'Well....yes..,' she mumbled, as he pulled her arm. Again, she stared at her walking stick.

As they reached the door, the old woman looked at Daniel.

'But..,' she said.

Daniel opened the door and took a deep breath.

'Hmmmm....breathe in the air, lady.'

'Well, I.....,' she said, as she stumbled a few steps past the shop door and lost her balance.

Daniel winced as the postman appeared at the door holding her walking stick. She gripped the head of the stick tightly, looked at the postman with equal disgust and hobbled off down the street muttering something about the government and her dodgy leg.

'It's *all* the government's fault, don't you know,' said Daniel in a squeaky old voice.

Daniel held back a few moments to watch the old lady hobble down the street and sat back at the table with a satisfied look on his face.

'Never miss an opportunity do you?' said the postman.

'Hey,' said Daniel as he pulled the soggy cigarette out of his espresso, 'I was doing her a favour. Couldn't you see how upset she was?' And with that, Daniel placed the wet cigarette in his mouth - its end relighting by itself. He sucked in the cigarette's fumes and presented a broad grin that clearly irritated the postman.

The postman played another move, knight to pawn, looking up at the waitress. He formed an invisible camera with his hands and pretended to take a photo. A faint shutter clicked in the background.

'How childish...,' said Daniel.

The postman shrugged.

Daniel turned to the mirror on the wall, between the bookcase and the payment counter, licked his fingers and brushed his hands through his dark wavy hair.

'Vanity. Such a killer,' he said, as he pictured the animated images of a woman driving a car through

Cambridge, putting her lipstick on in the car's rear view mirror. She drove straight into a motorcyclist and knocked him over the bonnet of her car. Daniel witnessed the bike's occupant fly through the air in slow motion and crash to the ground with a thud.

'You're losing the game..,' said Daniel, as he turned abruptly to the postman.

'Which one?' said the postman. As he glimpsed at the mirror, the postman slammed his hand down hard on the table.

'He's dead?' said the postman.

Daniel smiled, 'Well, not quite. Not yet.'

The postman stood up, scraping the chair noisily as it moved behind him. He pulled some coins from his pocket and threw them on the table.

'We're finished here,' said the postman, as he left the coffee shop.

Daniel saluted him and smiled.

'Sore loser,' said Daniel, looking up at the waitress.

The waitress noticed the chess board. 'The game..,' she said.

Daniel squinted.

'It's not finished,' she said.

'Oh, get back to your knitting,' said Daniel.

CHAPTER TEN

'What did you make of all that?' said Gemma. 'Well, they don't look like they're friends do they?' said Tim.

'No, not much. Why was Daniel so cruel to that old lady?'

'Who knows. He's just a nasty piece of work. Look what he did to my jacket,' he said, turning to show Gemma the rips on top of his jacket.

Gemma slid her finger down the scratch marks, and glanced at Daniel.

'What do you think he meant when he said history was going to rewrite itself?' she said.

'It all sounded very cryptic. Did you hear what the postman called him though? He called him *Deceiver.*'

'You and *your kind*, he said. Sounds like you were right about Daniel not being human. Something made the postman angry. I wonder what he meant when he asked if someone was dead. He said "he".'

'I don't know,' said Tim.

'And what was Daniel looking at in the mirror?'

'I couldn't see anything. But Gemma, don't you see. Maybe the postman is on our side after all. It's obvious he *isn't* a postman. So what if the compass really is from him? The text messages too. What if he's trying to help?'

'But if he knows what happened to your mum, why wouldn't he just tell you? I mean, why send you a compass?'

'Maybe he thinks I wouldn't believe him. Imagine. If Daniel isn't even human, who knows how believable the truth is. I mean. This is the real world. Everyone knows that there are no such things as monsters. This isn't Twilight. Vampires, werewolves, they're not real. So how can a man change into a bird? The fact is, he did.'

'Okay, let's say you're right. Let's say he did give you the compass.'

Tim nodded.

'Why wait? I mean, your mum's been missing for over a year now.'

'I know. It doesn't make sense when you put it that way.'

Gemma tapped her fingers on the table. 'When did you have your dream?'

'Last night. Wait, no, it was Wednesday night.'

'And the postman? When did he deliver the compass?'

'Well...the next morning.'

'Thursday you mean? Straight after your dream?'

Tim scratched his head. 'Now that you mention it, yes.'

'And your painting. The one you painted in art club. That was the *same* dream, right?'

'Yes, part of it anyway.'

Gemma pointed to the picture of the map on her camera. 'And now this?'

Tim ran his hands through his hair. 'I know. It all sounds crazy doesn't it?'

'That's one word for it. But this. It's real. I can see it. You can see it. If you are meant to find anything at all, then this map *must* mean something.'

'I guess so. But the compass is trying to take me somewhere too. It must be. When I followed the compass I found this old man inside a TV set.'

'Come on, Tim. Men who change into birds. Old men in TV sets?'

'I know how it sounds.'

'So who's the old man? What happened?'

'I was following the compass and stopped by Currys. I was watching the TVs in the window when this old man appeared on one of the screens. At first I thought it was some kind of demonstration. But then he started to reach out of the TV set.'

'Reach out?'

'Yes, like he was real. He made a kaleidoscope with glass from the shop window and gave it to me.'

'You really have quite an imagination, Tim,' she said.

'You don't believe me?'

'So where's the kaleidoscope now?'

'Nowhere. I mean it's gone.'

'Gone where?'

'It disappeared. I mean, it melted. On my bed.'

'Melted?'

'Yes, I don't know why, but it melted.'

Gemma sighed, and turned to her camera. 'You do see how surreal all this sounds don't you?'

'Surreal sums it up nicely.'

'And talking of surreal, it all seems to start with your dream.'

'You think so?'

'Yes, think about it. It's like your dream was a trigger for everything that's happened.'

'But how could it be? I mean, a dream's a dream. It's not reality.'

'Your dream is trying to tell you something, Tim. Whether it's what happened to your mum or not, I don't know. Is it the first time you've had that dream?'

'Well sort of.'

'What do you mean "sort of"?'

'They've always been blurry before. This was the first time I could see everything. You know, clearly.'

'And when did you start having them?'

'These really weird dreams started over a year ago.'

'After your mum disappeared?'

'Yes, about that time. This whole year has been tough. You know. What with the police telling us to expect the worst.'

Gemma stroked Tim's hand. 'Of course, I understand.'

'Something Daniel said to me last night. Something I remember.'

'Yes?'

'He asked me if I felt different.'

'That's a strange thing to ask.'

'That's what I thought. But I've been thinking. There was something that made me *feel* different.'

Gemma nodded, 'Feel different?'

'I had this strange feeling when I looked into the kaleidoscope. I mean, it was more than a kaleidoscope. It made me feel. Made me feel *different*.'

'Different how?'

'I don't know how to explain.'

'Try...'

'Kind of warm inside. Positive. Confident. Like I could do anything. Like all my worries had....gone.'

Gemma rubbed her chin.

'What?' he said.

'It's probably nothing.'

'Go on, what is it?'

'Something like that happened to me. Something similar.'

'When?'

'Just before I started to go through the paintings last night. I saw your painting. It made me feel, you know, warm inside. The same in the art club too.'

'Really?'

'Yes, something about it...lifted my spirit.'

'But isn't that just what art does?' he said.

'I know what you're trying to say. But now I think about it, it was more than that. It's more than just artistic curiosity.'

'Then everything is connected. Somehow.'

'Hmm..connected, maybe that's it.'

Tim shrugged.

'Remember how the others reacted to your painting?'

'They were just making compliments.'

'What was it Chloe said. "On top of the world"?'

'Something like that,' he said.

'Tim, think about it. If your painting really has this effect. And you felt that *same* feeling from the kaleidoscope...'

'You mean, someone is trying to show me how my paintings make people feel?'

'It's no more crazy than anything else you've told me today.'

'Who though?'

'Well, if the postman is on our side. Maybe it's him, maybe he's your man in the TV,' said Gemma.

'The man in the TV, he didn't look anything like the postman. No, Gemma, that's not it. Anyway, why would someone want me to know how my paintings make people feel?'

'Maybe you're special. Maybe someone wants you to *know* your special.'

'Why not just tell me then?'

'Would you believe someone if they told you?'

'Probably not before. But now I'd believe pretty much anything.' He looked up.

'What is it?'

'Something else I remembered. Something Daniel said. He said he sensed danger in me. Why would he say that?'

'Danger. Hmmm. So he sees you as some kind of threat?'

'How could I be a threat to him?' Tim looked down.

Gemma rubbed his arm. 'We'll figure this out. Don't worry.'

'The only real leads we've got at the moment are the compass and the map.' He picked the compass up from the table. 'And it's not glowing, so we should go and figure out where this map takes us. Come on. Let's get going.'

Gemma nodded and they left the coffee shop.

CHAPTER ELEVEN

Addenbrooke's Hospital, Cambridge.

Sat on the side of the bed, Daniel observed the wires and monitors attached to the man who lay there. For a few seconds, Daniel replayed the slow motion footage in his head, picturing once more the image of the motorcyclist as he flew over the bonnet of the car.

Daniel leaned towards the motorcyclist's ear and whispered, 'who's been a naughty boy then.....'

He placed his hand over the motorcyclist's forehead and held his hand. As he gripped the man's hand tighter, a light spark shot around Daniel's fingers.

'Not long now,' said Daniel, as the man's eyes started to close.

The monitor began to beep erratically and the green line straightened in the middle of the screen.

As the doors burst open, a small army of doctors and nurses rushed to the aid of the motorcyclist.

'Get *him* out of here,' one of the doctors shouted, pointing at Daniel. Two of the male nurses led Daniel out of the room.

Daniel watched through the window on the door as they tried to resuscitate the motorcyclist. Observing the monitor, he whistled the tune "Always look on the bright side of life" as it continued to flatline.

He turned his head around. 'Just before you draw your *terminal* breath,' he said, smiling at one of the female nurses who could see him through the window.

'Time of death. 10:15am,' said the doctor.

After the doctors and nurses left the motorcyclist, Daniel swaggered over to the bed. The motorcyclist was motionless, lifeless.

He glanced at the motorcyclist and took his hand. Clasping it tightly, he reached with his free hand to pull the monitor closer. A stream of light glowed around the motorcyclist's arm. Light flowed like a bolt of lightning from his arm, through Daniel's body. The monitor's black screen fizzled. For an instant, the monitor's screen became pure white, then a blur of coloured motion.

Memories from the motorcyclist's life flashed in short bursts on the monitor. His fights in the pub... petty crime in one town and another. Victims of those who bought his drugs...and images of a decadent lifestyle.

Daniel breathed in sharply, shaking slightly from the static electricity that surrounded him, gripping the man's hand until his own hand went blue.

A nail cracked - a trickle of blood ran over the motorcyclist's hand.

'How wonderfully unenlightened you were...Gary Brown,' he whispered, as the images continued on the monitor. A car raced onto the screen. A loud smash. The bike flew through the air, swerved and smashed into a lamppost as the man rolled over and curled into a ball by the pavement.

The monitor switched off.

Bright light around Daniel's body stopped glowing and Daniel let go of the man's hand, leaving it slightly blackened. Daniel's own fingernails looked darker. Rougher.

He savoured the last living memories of Gary Brown, before getting up and walking out of the hospital.

His work was done.

CHAPTER TWELVE

Tim stood a few metres away from the Great Gate, the main entrance to Trinity College. 'Do you think that's meant to keep us out, or them in?' he said.

Gemma shrugged. 'It's hard to say. Hey, isn't that Henry the Eighth above the coat of arms?'

Tim squinted. 'It looks like him. Why do you think it has two doors, look?' he said, observing that the entrance had a small wooden oval door close to a much larger one.

'Maybe the bigger gate is for those big heads...,' said Gemma, smirking.

Tim smiled and turned to Gemma. 'Do you have the print out of the map?'

'I thought I gave it to you?'

'Let me see,' said Tim, as he rummaged through his pockets. 'Hang on, what's this?' He pulled a small cellophane bag out from the inside pocket of his leather jacket and held it up.

'Powder?'

Tim slapped his head. 'No! Not powder. Drugs!'

'Drugs?'

'Yes, I told you earlier about those thugs. I had a run in. Outside the pub. These fellas turned up in a car trying to sell. You know. Drugs.'

'Tim!'

'Hey, don't look at me like that. I didn't buy them!'

Gemma sighed.

'It must have been the Goth. You know, from art club.'

'He was there?'

'Yes, I thought he was trying to help me. Don't you see Gemma. He planted them.'

'Why would he do that?'

'I don't know. To get me into trouble?'

'I think you're getting paranoid now, Tim.'

'What if Dad had found it? He'd kill me.'

'If you're right, then it looks like you can't trust anyone, Tim.'

'What if he's with Daniel? What if he's one of them? You know, what was it the postman called Daniel?'

'Deceiver, wasn't it?'

'That's it. What if he's a Deceiver? Think about it, Gemma. I was beginning to think he was okay. But he really has tricked me. That's what they do.'

Gemma nodded. 'The old woman in the coffee shop. Daniel started out being nice to her.'

'Yes, but it was all a con,' said Tim, putting the bag back in his pocket.

'I wonder what the Deceivers want.'

Tim shrugged. 'First the bird in maths. Then Daniel. It looks like they want me. They want to kill me.'

'Don't you think they would have done that by now, if that was their plan?'

'I don't know,' he said.

Tim slapped his head. 'The bird in maths. That was the first time I saw it. But something else happened. I thought it was strange at the time. Patrick, he answered one of the questions wrong. I mean, a real easy one. What if the bird distracted him? You know, on purpose.'

'What do you mean "the bird in maths"?' said Gemma.

'We had a maths test and this bird smashed into the window. It looked just like the one Daniel changed into. I think that's what they do, Gemma. They put people off. Distract them. Deceive them. Just like Daniel did in the coffee shop. Just like the bird did in maths.'

'It sounds like you're making up some kind of conspiracy theory,' she said.

'I don't know, if this Goth is one of them too, who knows how many of them there are?' He reached into a pocket inside his jacket. 'I was beginning to think I'd lost it. At least we've still got the map, look.'

They sat on the grass opposite the stack of bikes that lined the path to the smaller wooden door.

'It looks a bit like a castle from here, doesn't it?' said Gemma, looking up at the Great Gate.

Tim nodded. 'Yes, they must be fighting to keep people out. Anyway, how are we going to get in?' he said. 'It's not like we can go and knock on the front door.'

'Good question. We still don't know where to go. Not exactly, anyway.'

'Look at this part. It's got to be one of the buildings in here, one of the rooms,' said Tim, turning to the map.

'There are so many buildings here though. Where to start?'

'Look,' he said, 'what if these are windows here? There's a whole row of them.'

'I remember coming on a school trip here a few years ago,' said Gemma. 'I know there was a chapel with lots of windows. Oh yes, and I remember a small courtyard with arches all the way down. I think it was a library.'

Tim slapped his head. 'Library! Of course. In my dream, I was flying through Cambridge on my front garden.'

'Flying on your front garden?' said Gemma, with a smirk.

'What I wanted to say was, I remember going through a window. I remember a building. I think it might have been a library.'

'That must be it then.'

'Can you remember where it is? I mean, from your school trip?'

'I don't think we could go through the main entrance. Let's go find the porter. He'll know,' she said.

'Is it even open to the public?'

'Well it was when I visited. But it's term time now, I don't know.'

'He must be a porter, look he's wearing a bowler hat,' said Tim, as the porter strolled down the pathway from the main street.

'Excuse me,' said Gemma, turning to the porter.

'Yes, Miss?'

'Can you tell me where the library is?'

'You mean Wren library, Miss?'

'I...I think so.'

'You can get to it from Garret Hostel Lane,' said the porter.

'Which way from here?' said Tim.

'Just follow the street to the right here,' said the porter. 'Right down Trinity Lane, follow the street round and make another right on to Garrett Hostel Lane. You'll see a bridge – just make a right before the bridge and that will take you to an entrance where you can get access to the library.' He glanced at his watch. 'One of my colleagues should be there to guide you, by the time you get there."

'Got that?' said Gemma, glancing at Tim.

Tim nodded. 'The library's open?' said Tim, turning to the porter.

'Yes, it opened about a half hour ago. You best be on your way, because it's only open for a couple of hours.'

'No time for War and Peace then,' said Gemma, smirking.

The porter smiled.

'Don't we have to pay?' said Tim.

'No, Sir. That's one thing around here that you don't have to pay for.'

＝╌ ╌＝

Wren Library, Cambridge.

'Wow,' said Tim, 'this is huge. There must be *millions* of books in here.'

He admired the archways inset on the higher walls, either side of the colourful stained glass window at the far end of the room. The light streamed in through the windows.

'It hasn't changed a bit,' said Gemma, as she passed the wooden bookcases - stacked up on each side like a row of dominoes, lightly brushing the wood with her hand.

Tim noticed the chequered floor. 'Feels like we're pieces on a chess board. So, where should we start then Gemma?' he said.

She took the map from Tim and spun it around a few times.

'We don't even know what we're looking for,' said Tim. He surveyed the depths of the enormous library and sighed.

'Yes we do!' said Gemma, '...we're in a library, so we must be looking for a book....left or right?' she said, switching her head between the two rows of bookcases on either side of the corridor.

'Let's toss for it,' he said, flipping a coin in the air. 'Heads for left, tails for right. Your call.'

'Tails,' said Gemma.

'Sorry, Gemma, it's heads,' he said, taking his hand off the coin.

Tim turned to his left and strolled down the central corridor.

'These lines on either side,' said Gemma pointing at the map, 'they must be the bookcases. And these marks, must be the busts look,' she pointed at one of the white marble-looking busts sat on a wooden base at waist height. 'Famous authors, maybe?'

Tim shrugged and turned to the map. 'If you're right, then we're on the wrong side,' said Tim, turning the map around.

They crossed the chequered floor to the other side.

'It must be this bookcase look. The one with the circled cross,' said Tim, leading the way to the last but one bookshelf. 'If we're reading this right, it should be somewhere on this bookcase. But look, there must be, what, nine...ten shelves,' he said, looking up at the dark mahogany bookcase, '..and God knows how many books. We can't possibly go through all of them.'

'But look,' she said. 'There's a smaller marking. You see those brush strokes. There's a faint mark on the second line. The second shelf surely?' she said, pointing at the mark on the map.

Tim shrugged.

'The original Winnie the Pooh's in this library, you know,' said Gemma.

'I hope he's on a leash,' said Tim.

Tim felt a sharp pinch on his arm.

'Tim. Come on, be serious....so...I'll start from the left, you start from the right,' and with that Gemma pulled the first book from the second shelf.

Tim did the same on the right side.

'Chaucer,' said Gemma, flipping through the pages.

'Carroll,' said Tim, pulling out *Alice in Wonderland*. 'Anything inside?'

Tim flipped the pages. 'No..nothing here. Although...'

'Yes...yes...?' said Gemma.

'It's so worn...looks like it's the original!'

Gemma swished her hand to one side as if she was shooing away an unwanted fly.

Tim took out a second book. Gemma did the same.

Then a third.

'This is hopeless,' said Tim, 'we don't even know what we're looking for.'

Glancing towards Tim as she reached for the fourth book, Gemma screamed.

Tim spun around to see what had happened and dropped the fourth book on the floor.

Right there, in front of Gemma, was an elderly man. He was dressed in an oversized green woolly cardigan and checked trousers that were so short you could see his bright yellow and orange socks.

'Where did you come from?' said Gemma, as she gathered her composure.

Tim stared at the man. He looked as old as the library. He must be the librarian.

'Can I...', said the librarian.

Tim glanced at Gemma. He could tell that she wanted to help the librarian spit the words out.

'Help you?' said the librarian, finally gathering enough strength.

'You gave me quite a fright,' said Gemma, tugging the fourth book close to her chest.

'Slippers,' said the librarian.

'What's that?' said Gemma.

'It's these slippers of mine. Quiet as a mouse, I am,' he said, pointing down at his feet - covered in a pair of old worn out slippers that looked more like road-kill than foot warmers.

Crack!

'What was that?' shouted Tim. He turned. A big black bird smacked its beak against one of the arched windows. Tim flinched. 'Where did it go? Gemma, it was one of *those* birds. I'm sure of it.'

'I didn't see anything,' said Gemma.

Tim turned to the librarian, but he just shrugged.

'Is this place always so creepy?' said Gemma, looking at the librarian.

The librarian didn't answer and hobbled off down the corridor.

'He was a barrel of laughs wasn't he...come on, let's carry on, before the bird comes back,' said Tim.

Tim tugged at the fifth book and found the book was a bit stiff. He tugged again.

Gemma did the same.

Tim heard a noise and felt something hit his feet. He jumped backwards.

An opening in the bookcase, just below the first shelf, revealed a small wooden box.

'Look Gemma!'

Tim crouched down to pick up the box.

'A secret compartment. Go on, open it then.'

'Just imagine how long this has been hidden here,' said Tim as he opened the box. 'Hey, there's a book in here,' he said as he blew the dust off the front cover.

A thick black spider scurried across the cover, its hairy legs kicking up dust until it reached the other side. It turned from side to side as if it was going to cross a road and disappeared inside.

'It's handwritten. Full of...maths,' he said, flipping through the tainted yellow pages.

'What kind of maths?' said Gemma.

'God knows,' said Tim, 'it's all Greek to me.'

'Nothing about your mum then?'

'No, nothing.' A shadow from the large stained glass window above the central corridor caught Tim's eye. 'Did you see that?'

'What?'

'Something outside. I saw something pass the window up there. I think it was that bird, again.'

'Outside the stained window you mean?'

'Yes, that one there.' Tim rubbed his chin as he studied the image on the window. 'Newton! Didn't he study at Cambridge?' He glanced at Gemma for confirmation and turned to the stained glass window, admiring the large oval shaped glass. Isaac Newton etched into its colourful design.

'Yes....Newton. You're right. I think he was at Cambridge,' said Gemma.

'What if...?' said Tim, '..what if this book, what if it's Newton's...fourth law?'

'Fourth law?'

'Yes. I'm no expert, but everyone knows Newton's three laws.'

'Everyone?'

Tim paused. 'Well, everyone *except* you, maybe!'

'Let's not jump to conclusions, Tim.'

'Think about it. We've just found a book that's been hidden for God knows how long. Hundreds of years? And it's hardly a coincidence that we're in the same college where Newton studied is it?'

'But why a fourth law? A law about what?' said Gemma.

'Well, from what I can remember, his first three laws were all about motion,' said Tim. 'You must have heard of "for every action there is an equal and opposite reaction"?'

Tim grabbed the book and the box and pushed them towards each other, like two trains about to hit each other, then pulled them apart after they almost collided.

'That sounds familiar. But....well...it still doesn't explain why he would have a fourth law. Or...why he would hide it.'

'True. But look at these formulas. There must be something special about them. Otherwise why would they be hidden?' said Tim.

He passed the book to Gemma and, while she browsed through the worn pages, he felt inside the box.

'Wait, Gemma,' he said. 'There's something here. Another box inside.' He pulled the top of the box off. 'Loose papers full of names, dates. Lots of them.'

Before Tim could study them further, Gemma distracted him, dropping the book on the floor, forcing it to slide into the central corridor.

Gemma screamed.

A large black bird waddled across the chequered floor. It limped towards the book, close to where they stood.

Tim froze. 'Don't move, Gemma.'

'Look how it's walking. Birds don't walk like that.'

Tim nodded as the bird pecked at the book.

'You can't let it take the book, Tim, do something.'

Tim pulled a book from the shelf and threw it at the bird. The book slid across the floor, missing the bird completely.

The bird flicked its head towards Tim, then twisted towards Gemma, before grabbing the book in its open beak.

Tim dived and slid across the chequered floor. He smashed into the bird and tugged at the book, trying to pry it from the bird's enormous beak.

'Go on, Tim, get it out.'

Tim pulled the book away, as the bird opened the full span of its wings and began to flap them wildly.

Whoosh.

The book fell to the floor again and opened up on the last page.

Tim inched back on the floor as the bird charged at him. The bird turned sharply and ripped the last page out of the book and gripped it in its beak. The rip echoed around the walls of the library.

Tim felt like his mind was playing tricks. Images of a bird tugging at a book sprang into his head. Pulling at the paper. Familiar images. Images from his dream.

'Quick! It's getting away,' said Gemma, pulling Tim up off the floor.

Tim reached for the bird's claws, but it was already too high. It flew across the length of the library and out of the main entrance.

'Where's the librarian gone? Surely he can hear it?' said Tim.

'I'm not so sure, Tim,' said Gemma. 'He seemed to be as deaf as a post. Come on. Let's go. Get the book. You better put those other books back where we found them.'

Tim nodded and put the books back in their place. The secret compartment closed as if it had never existed. He picked up the box with the papers and passed it to Gemma, as she put the book in her handbag.

They darted to the entrance.

'Just a moment, you two,' said a voice.

Tim glanced at Gemma.

'You haven't signed the guest book,' said the librarian, as he pointed down at a large guest book resting on a finely engraved wooden block.

'Oh....yes...yes..of course,' said Gemma, as she scribbled her name in the guest book.

The librarian stared at Tim.

'Oh....right,' said Tim, taking the pen off Gemma and adding his name to the guest book.

The librarian nodded. 'Did you find what you were looking for?'

'Yes...yes...I think so,' said Tim, as he pushed Gemma ahead of him.

They ran from the college grounds and out of the gate.

Gemma stopped.

'What's up with you, come on?'

'Just look at that,' said Gemma, admiring the view of the students punting on the river ahead of them.

'No time for that. The bird, remember? We've got to get away from here.'

As Tim sprinted away from the college gate, he knocked an artist's easel over.

'Hey!' said the artist, kneeling down to pick up her paints.

'Sorry,' said Tim, '...nice painting!'

At the exit, Tim spun left, then right towards the bridge.

'We can get a taxi near Green Street, come on this way,' said Gemma, as they took a left.

They didn't stop running until they got past Green Street and hailed a taxi.

The taxi left the roadside and headed to Gemma's house.

—✦ ✦—

Leaving the driver with a crisp new ten pound note, they ran into Gemma's house, straight to the dining area.

Gemma took the book and box out of her handbag and put them on the table.

Tim skimmed through the book, occasionally stopping to observe the drawings in the margin.

'Tim, the chances of this being anything at all to do with Newton are next to none. You seriously think we're the first people to see this? Whatever this is,' said Gemma.

'But you saw how we found it. Who's gone to all that trouble to hide it? Why is it so important?'

Tim continued to read through the book while Gemma inspected the box and started to spread the paper notes out over the table.

'These notes,' she said. 'They look like some kind of prison records. Names, dates, crimes. They must be hundreds of years old. Hey, there are some initials here. E.N.?' she said, pointing at the initials engraved on the box.

'What's that?' said Tim.

'Here....initials on the box. I didn't notice them earlier.'

'So it *is* Newton then?' he said, putting the book down and tapping his fingers on the box lightly. 'Maybe it's not an E.'

'Isaac Newton,' said Gemma, 'I..N.'

'Maybe it's an old fashioned "E"...or...maybe Isaac wasn't his first name?' said Tim.

'You're really set on this Newton idea aren't you? I'm going upstairs for a minute. See what Uncle Google can tell us about Newton.'

Tim turned to the papers from the box, spread out over the dining table. Hand written prison records. Was Newton visiting prisons? Why would he do that?

'Sir Isaac Newton. Born, 25 December 1642. Died, 20 March 1727. According to Wikipedia anyway,' said Gemma, calling out from upstairs.

'What if it's a title of some kind....esquire maybe?' shouted Tim.

Gemma marched down the stairs and sat back at the dining table.

'Esquire? I don't think so. Face it, Tim, it's not Newton.'

Tim sighed as he shuffled the loose papers on the table. 'Too much information. We need to filter it down.'

'What do you suggest?'

'I know. Sticky notes. Do you have any?'

'I don't think so. No, wait, my dad might have some in his study,' she said as she darted out of the living room.

Tim skimmed through the book and stopped on a page in the middle. 'Gemma, come look at this.'

'Just a minute, I'm just looking for these sticky notes....ah...found some.'

Tim glanced at Gemma as she came back into the room, 'great, pass them here.'

'So what is it? What do you want me to look at?'

'Look!' said Tim, pointing at the drawing in the book's margin.

'It's a bird, isn't it?'

'Not just any bird, Gemma. It's one of them. Look at the beak.'

'So all this. Everything that's happening, goes back hundreds of years?'

Tim shrugged. 'Maybe even longer for all we know.' He ripped off a sticky note from the small pack. 'Pen?'

Gemma reached in the dresser and took out a couple of marker pens, and passed them to Tim.

'Here, give me one,' she said.

"Deceivers," Tim scribbled onto the first note.

"Library.

Prison notes.

Newton.

Dream.

Painting."

Gemma nodded. 'I see. I see what you're doing. A proper little detective you are...' She tapped the pen on her forehead, picked up the "Newton" note and added a question mark.

"E.N.," wrote Gemma, placing it next to Newton.

Tim continued to write out the clues:

"Kaleidoscope.

Postman.

Daniel.

Goth.

Mum.

Compass."

Tim picked up "Goth" and "Daniel" and placed them under "Deceivers", pushing them to the right side of the table. 'Bad stuff on this side, good stuff on the left, unknown in the middle. Okay?'

Gemma nodded and placed the book in the middle of the table. 'Unknown, right?'

'Yes, that's right.'

"Old man in TV.

Fourth Law?

Birds."

'There, have we missed anything?' said Tim.

'I can't think of anything else. I'll put the papers here?' she said, hovering over the middle of the table.

'Yes, next to the book.'

Tim picked up the paper on top of the pile. 'Handwriting Gemma! Check Newton's handwriting,' he said, passing her the loose sheet from the top, 'there must be some samples of his writing on the Internet. Somewhere.'

'I'm on it,' she said, running back upstairs.

Tim picked up the "Kaleidoscope" sticky note and hovered between the middle and the left side, placing it on the left. 'Good....I hope,' he muttered.

'Newton's T's curl round on the left side. They're not the same,' said Gemma.

'I can hardly hear you,' said Tim.

Gemma thudded downstairs and marched back into the dining area. 'It's *definitely* not Newton,' she said, 'his T's curl to the left. So who on earth is E.N?'

'I think we have to go back to the library, Gemma.'

'What for?'

'To find out who E.N. is of course. And to figure out what *this* is all about,' he said, pointing at the formulas in the book.

'Someone went to a lot of trouble to hide this box. But why? All I can see are equations and prison records. Why hide them? What's the big secret?'

'What about the dates on the records?' said Tim. 'It must give us some idea of what period we're talking about. It might have been a student at the university.'

'If we can assume he was at the university,' said Gemma.

'We're in Cambridge, Gemma. I'd say that's pretty likely.'

Tim sifted through the prison records and shouted out the years as Gemma scribbled them on the sticky notes.

"1695.

1696."

'1696? Gemma, when was the Great Plague?' he said.

'1666 wasn't it?'

'Sounds about right. Or was that the Great Fire of London?' He paused. 'Did the Plague ever reach Cambridge?'

'Not that I know of. Although the university was shut down around that time, I seem to remember reading. Maybe it did reach Cambridge.'

"1697.

1698.

1699."

'These notes go on and on for years,' said Tim, 'the last one I can find is 1725.'

Gemma picked up the sticky notes she'd written out and screwed them up, scribbling on a fresh sticky note:

"1695 – 1725"

Tim picked it up and placed it in the middle of the table.

'Thirty years of records, all crammed in this box. What does it all mean?' said Gemma.

'So much dedication. Whoever it was, they were definitely a stickler for detail,' he said.

'So let's say our man..*or woman*..was studying at the university in 1695 or any of the other years. How does that really help us? It doesn't tell us what this formula is about.'

Tim jerked his pen as he was about to add the question mark to "Great Plague".

'Was that your door bell?' he said.

Gemma nodded and went to the front door.

'There's no one here,' she said. 'Oh, but wait, there's something on the doormat.'

'Strange,' she said, as she entered the dining area, 'there was no one there...only this parcel.'

'You think we should open it?' said Tim. 'The last time I got a parcel, well you know, I got this compass.'

Gemma sighed. 'Feels too light for a compass.'

He pulled at the paper wrapping. Once the wrapping was off, he opened the cardboard box. At first the box appeared to be empty. But there, in the corner, was something stuck to the side.

'What is it, Tim?'

'It's a feather. A bird's feather.'

As his fingers touched it, he flinched.

'What's wrong?'

He let go of the feather and let it fall to the carpet.

'Cold....it's *so* cold,' said Tim.

Crackle.

'What was that?' said Gemma.

'It seemed to come from upstairs. It's getting closer, listen.'

Looking straight at Tim, Gemma nodded towards the living room door. 'Look,' she said, '..shadows.'

As a dark shape grew larger on the wall, Gemma closed her eyes.

'Gemma!' said Tim.

'What is it, what is it?'

Tim pointed down towards the floor.

'Holy cow. You scared the *beefburgers* out of me,' said Gemma, turning to her cat, Einstein.

'Don't you mean b*ergeebers*?' said Tim.

Gemma smiled. 'I know what I mean,' and hit Tim's arm. 'Don't scare me like that.'

'Hey, it wasn't me. It was your stupid cat.'

'Einstein! You made us jump!' she said, reaching down to pick him up.

Crackle.

'There it is again, it sounds like it's coming from the kitchen now,' said Gemma.

Tim took the book off the table and put it in his pocket. 'We should go and see what it is,' he said, leading the way to the kitchen.

'Look at the window!' said Gemma, as the glass on the kitchen door started to frost over.

'How's that possible?' said Tim.

'Quick, let's get out of here. You've got the book?'

Tim patted his pocket.

'What about the prison notes?'

'They're on your table.'

Gemma sighed. 'No time then, come on, let's go.' She was first out the back door, closely followed by Tim.

The glass pane on the door frosted over completely as Tim let go of the door handle and Einstein shot out of the cat flap onto the back garden.

'That was close,' she said, as the whole house was engulfed in a frosty, ice-like substance.

'Look at that stuff. It looks like it's....glowing,' said Gemma.

Tim raced down the garden to the back gate and just before slamming it shut, took a last look at the house, with Gemma at his side.

Stood at the back door, was a man dressed in a long, dark black coat. He was looking down, lighting a cigarette.

'It's Daniel,' said Gemma. 'He's frozen the whole house!'

'The feather...in the parcel...it was his. Run, Gemma!' shouted Tim.

CHAPTER THIRTEEN

'How did he find us? What does he want?' said Gemma, as they stopped for breath three streets away.

'Isn't it obvious? He wants the book, Gemma.'

'So where now?'

Tim flipped open the compass.

No glow.

Tim frowned and tapped his fingers on the compass as he pondered, then flipped it shut.

Out of the corner of his eye, he saw something move in the hedge in front of one of the houses. It was too fast to make it out. Before he could put the compass in his trouser pocket, he became aware of a flap above and looked up.

Nothing.

Something hit the base of his back, and the compass dropped from his light grip. He felt a sharp pain in his palm, as a bird's beak grabbed a small hook on the compass and shot ahead of him, rising quickly to the tree above.

Tim rubbed the pain on his back and moved closer to the tree, when Einstein appeared. Einstein jumped onto the wall in front of the house and clawed his way up the tree trunk to the first low hanging branch. The bird lifted one of its wings and tried to protect the compass as Einstein lashed out. The shiny metallic compass flew out of the bird's beak into the air as Einstein's claws scratched the left side of the bird's head. The bird tumbled down the tree, bouncing off branches – just managing to regain flight when it was inches from the ground.

Tim dived on the small patch of grass in front of the hedge and caught the compass with both hands, close to his chest. He brushed himself down and looked up as Einstein jumped from the tree.

'Quick, it's coming,' shouted Gemma, as she yanked him aside.

Tim felt the bird's wing brush against his shoulder. Noticing a broken branch on the grass, he picked it up and made like a baseball player, whacking the bird hard as it lunged towards him – sending it hurtling into a wheelie bin.

Instinctively, Tim sprinted down the street, tightly gripping the compass - Gemma trailing behind. They didn't stop running until they reached a playground on Green End Road – where a couple of children were swinging on a large black wheel by a sandpit.

'I can't see it,' said Gemma, panting for breath.

Tim sighed. 'I think I got it. I mean, I really hit it hard.'

Tim felt a vibration in his pocket and reached for the compass.

'Gemma look, it's glowing. Now do you believe me?'

Gemma took the compass from Tim's hand and nodded.

'We need to continue up here,' said Tim. 'It looks like it's getting brighter. Maybe we're close now.'

'Close to what?' said Gemma, as she passed the compass back.

'To wherever it wants to take us.'

'But they're just housing estates here.'

'What if Mum's being held in a house here?'

Gemma shrugged. 'Come on, let's keep going,' she said, glancing at the compass.

They followed its lead, turning on to Laxton Way, where Tim stopped.

'Look Gemma, what is that? A clearing over there?'

'There's a signboard, look. Let's go and see.'

'Bramblefields nature reserve. It wants us to go through here look.'

Tim spotted a clearing and noticed that the compass felt warm in his hand. The blue glow became brighter and brighter and the needle started shaking violently.

Tim crouched down and put the compass on the grass.

He moved the compass from one spot to another, until he found a spot that turned the blue glow on the compass into a rainbow of colour.

'Can you see that?' he said. 'Look at the colours Gemma! This is it!'

'Hey, calm down,' said Gemma, holding his arm.

'I mean, look at the compass. It's going crazy. Whatever we're meant to find, Gemma, it's here.'

'Underground?'

Tim shrugged, reached for a small twig and pushed it into the soil. The twig hit something after just a few seconds.

'It's...a box,' said Tim, scooping the soil away, revealing a container caked in a clay-like mud, no larger than a jewellery box.

He picked up the box and skipped to the nearby pond.

'Better get some of this mud off,' he said, carefully washing the box in the water.

'Look at the engravings,' said Gemma. 'It's awesome.'

Tim wiped the metallic plate on the front. It had an intricate design engraved on its cover. One side of the box was slightly indented, with a small rectangular area and two small slits inside.

He took the compass in one hand and held the box in the air with the other. Slowly, Tim spun the box around and inspected each side.

'Look at these grooves,' said Gemma.

'Hmm...I wonder,' said Tim. He took the box and placed it on the ground by the pond - pushing the compass against the two grooves. The compass snapped against the box – a perfect fit.

Tim stared at the box, now firmly locked in place with the compass.

'What's happening?' said Gemma, as a rainbow-like glow on the compass became brighter and a faint hum came from inside the box.

'Yes, I can hear it too.'

The compass lid closed and disconnected itself from the grooves on the box.

Tim picked up the compass, put it inside his pocket and took a step backwards.

A series of mechanical sounds stirred in the box and its top expanded into five layers of square wooden plates, each offset by a few degrees. The plates spun, each at different speeds. As the plates spun faster and faster, they split open and revealed a round hole. A bright, white light shot out of the hole.

Tim gasped, his mouth opened....and he reached out towards the box – drawn in like a magnet. He had to touch it. He didn't know why, but he had to.

Gemma tried to stop him and grabbed his side, as Tim picked up the box.

The mechanical clicks grew louder and louder. Tim's fingers slowly reached into the light. His forefinger surrounded by static electricity. His whole body glowed. Sheets of coloured waves burst out of the box and erupted high into the air.

Tim remembered the kaleidoscope the old man in the TV set had given him, how it looked when it melted on his bed. The colours that surrounded him, the way they danced. It was just the same.

'I...I can't feel my legs,' said Gemma, 'what's happening? All I can see...are colours.'

And just like that, Tim and Gemma were gone.

CHAPTER FOURTEEN

Tim's hand twitched. Thank God. He was alive! As he regained consciousness he felt the box in his hand – now closed. The last thing he remembered was a vigorous display of colours dancing over him after he unlocked the box by the pond.

He turned to his side and saw Gemma lying motionless. Everything else around him a blur.

'Gemma? Gemma, are you okay?'

No answer.

As Tim focussed on his new surroundings, objects became clearer. Books. A small sofa. A dimly lit room.

He tapped the wooden floor with his shoe.

Gemma's eyes shot open. 'Is that a grandfather clock?' she said. 'Thirty minutes to twelve?'

'Where are we?' said Tim. 'It feels like we're in a museum. Look how dated everything is.'

'What's that noise?' said Gemma.

'I hear it too.'

They both spun around and came face to face with a young man, sitting at a desk. The man looked rough - his hair coffee brown. Stiff and messy. His chin dimpled, unshaven. He didn't look a day over twenty, except for those eyes, creased and puffy.

'Who's that?' said Tim.

'Shhh, he'll hear you.'

The man was scribbling words in a small book, sweat running down his brow. A drop of sweat fell to his book and hit the fresh ink, causing it to blur. With an almost vacant look, he tapped his fingers on the desk.

'He's looking straight at us, but it's like he can't see us,' said Tim.

Gemma approached the man and waved in front of his face. 'Look at his clothes. You won't find those in Next.'

No reaction.

She looked straight into the man's face. 'Hey, you, are you deaf?'

No reaction, again.

'He can't see us. He can't hear us,' said Gemma. 'This is crazy. What kind of place is this?'

Tim ran his hands over the books on the shelf next to the desk. 'We're in some kind of office, maybe his study,' said Tim.

Behind the man's desk, near the window, a small blackboard was covered in more scribblings and mathematical formulas. The man glanced at his silver pocket watch, pulling it from his beautifully tailored waistcoat. He wiped his brow with a crisp new handkerchief, his initials finely woven in black.

'Tim look! His initials,' said Gemma.

Tim skipped over to the desk. 'E.N.' said Tim, as he ran his fingers over the initials.

'Exactly, E.N,' said Gemma. *He* is E.N.'

'He doesn't look anything like Newton,' said Tim.

'No. No, he doesn't does he. I told you!'

'So who is he then?'

'That's what we have to find out.'

'Gemma look at the book he's writing in,' said Tim, pulling out his copy of the book from his jacket pocket. 'It's him. He's the writer. It's his book.'

'We need to find out who he is. Let's look around the room. There has to be something here with his name on it.'

'You're right. There must be something.'

Gemma started sifting through some papers in front of the bookcase. 'He's quite a messy worker, whoever he is.'

'Hey, hang on a minute, Gemma. What if he can see you holding those papers?' said Tim.

Gemma strolled over to the man and waved the papers in his face.

'Look. He can't see the papers. Whatever we're holding is invisible too,' she said.

'It's like we're here, but we're not here. So if he's the author, we must be in the 1600's.'

'Or the 1700's. Remember the prison notes we found? They spanned across the 1600's and 1700's.'

'So we've just travelled back in time?' said Tim, looking at the box in his hand.

'Well, it might explain why he can't see us.'

'True. But it's weird how everything still feels real here. I mean I can even smell the leather on his chair.'

'You better give me the box. I'll keep it safe,' said Gemma, putting it in her handbag.

Tim ran his fingers across a row of books on the bookshelf, before he reached down to a small table tucked away in the corner, near the blackboard.

'I've found an envelope,' he said.

'His name?'

'Yes, it's Edward.'

'Edward who?'

'Edward Noble.'

'Never heard of him.'

'But that's not all, Gemma.'

'Yes?'

'We're in Cambridge,' he said, turning the envelope around for Gemma to see.

Gemma approached the window behind Edward's desk and pulled back the curtain. 'It's too dark outside. I can hardly see a thing.'

'What's he doing working so late?' said Tim, looking back at the grandfather clock. 'It'll soon be midnight.'

'Look at his face, Tim.'

'It looks like he hasn't slept for a hundred years. He's been up for hours hasn't he?'

'Look, he's getting up, quick move.'

'Don't worry, he can't see us,' said Tim.

'Oh yes. I don't think I'm ever going to get used to this. Come on, let's follow him.'

Edward picked up the book, approached the coat stand in the hallway and put on a blue, embroidered frock coat. Opening the front door, he took a deep breath. He lingered for quite some time before he took his first step.

'He looks troubled. Like he's got the weight of the world on his shoulders,' said Gemma.

'Looks like it. But where's he going at this time of night?'

'We better follow him.'

Tim and Gemma followed closely, passing shops before they reached a fork in the road.

'It's so quiet out here,' said Gemma.

'Well, it's nearly midnight.'

Tim marvelled at their surroundings. Oil lamps every few houses. Not a single car in sight. It felt like he was on the set of a Charles Dickens period drama.

They followed Edward on to St Andrews Street.

'He just seems to be wandering, don't you think?' said Gemma.

'I know what you mean. It doesn't feel like he knows where he's going.'

'Who's that?' said Tim, noticing an old man sitting on the ground with his back against a wall. He stared at the old man. At first he thought it was a vagrant, but on closer inspection, the old man appeared to be too finely dressed.

'What's wrong? You look confused.' said Gemma.

'That man. That old man. He looks very familiar.'

'Familiar?'

Tim nodded. 'I'm sure I've seen him somewhere before.'

As Edward was about to pass the old man, the man turned to him.

'What's he doing?' said Gemma, as she watched the old man clasp Edward's hand tightly.

'I know what you seek,' said the old man, with a rough, raspy voice, as if he'd broken a vow of silence.

'Let go!' said Edward, as he tried to pull his hand away.

'It starts here,' said the old man, '...go to the bridewell.'

'Bridewell? What bridewell?' said Edward.

'This one,' said the old man, coughing violently. 'The Spinning House.' He looked up at the building in front of them and held his arms out, as if welcoming a family member into his house.

'What's a bridewell?' said Tim, looking over at Gemma.

'I'm not really sure. Although I've heard of the Spinning House. Haven't you?'

'No, I don't think so,' said Tim.

'I think the Spinning House used to be a prison. Like centuries ago. We studied it in history. It's hard to forget a name like that.'

'Who is that man? How can he know what Edward is looking for?'

'Maybe he's drunk. You know, just talking rubbish.'

'No, I don't think so. I can't help think I've seen his face before,' he said.

Gemma shrugged.

'What do you mean, old man?' said Edward.

'I know what you seek,' said the old man, again.

'Yes...yes...so you say,' said Edward. He turned to face the Spinning House. 'There's nothing in there but reprobates.'

The old man nodded vigorously, smiled and directed his head towards the door of the Spinning House.

'What choice do I have?' said Edward.

The old man smiled as he turned to the Spinning House. 'Hobson's choice....mathematician,' he mumbled under his breath.

'How do you know I'm a mathematician?' said Edward.

The man didn't answer, he just nodded his head towards the door again.

Gemma whispered to Tim, 'mathematician?'

'You don't have to whisper, remember?'

'Why is he looking at the door like that?'

'He's obviously wondering whether to go in.'

Edward moved closer to the large, oval wooden door. The door creaked open. Tim and Gemma followed behind.

'It's really cold in here,' said Tim.

A tall, grumpy looking man with a ghostly thin face stood in their way.

'Who are you? What are you doing here? Do you know what time it is?' said the man.

'Errr, well..,' said Tim.

Gemma tapped his shoulder. 'He's not talking to you. *Remember?*'

Tim could see Edward struggling to make a quick response.

Tugging at his waistcoat with both hands, Edward raised his head. 'My name is Edward Noble and I am here in an official capacity, on behalf of the university. We are conducting research into..,' he paused, took in his surroundings, then continued, '..into the statistical probability of losing one's social standing.'

'Do excuse me, sir' said the keeper, his voice becoming more refined and gracious, '..we get all sorts in here, and we rarely receive visits from...'

'No matter. Just guide me through this rat-infested hovel,' said Edward. He glanced at the large book sitting on the corner of the keeper's desk. 'Then I want to review the records,' said Edward.

'But sir. It's nearly midnight,' said the keeper.

'No matter. My research has no such constraints. Now, are you going to be a gentleman or not?'

'Certainly sir. I'm at your disposal,' said the keeper.

The keeper guided Edward on a tour of the building. Poorly dressed young girls were gathered in small groups. Small cells housing two beds and little else. Everything felt so hopeless inside these four walls. The whole place felt soulless.

Edward approached one of the girls. She couldn't have been more than fourteen or fifteen.

Tim and Gemma stood either side of the girl.

'You there...why are you here? What did you do?' said Edward.

'Isn't it a bit late for them to be up?' said Gemma.

'Shhhh! Let's listen,' said Tim, brushing his finger over his lips.

'Lost....lost my way, sir,' she said, looking for approval from the keeper.

'And not for the first time,' said the keeper. 'You see, sir, most of them end up back here.'

'Tell me,' said Edward, as he tapped his head with his forefinger in thought, '..how did you lose your way?'

'Not sure what you mean, sir,' she said.

'I mean, how did it start?' said Edward.

The girl looked down and mumbled. 'A voice, sir. A voice in my head.'

One of the other girls overheard and dropped the dish she was carrying. A loud, shattering crash echoed around the room as the dish broke into tiny pieces.

The keeper shook his head, 'voices...voices in my head sir,' he said, imitating her with a high pitched, uneducated tone.

Edward pulled out a book and scribbled inside.

'There's nothing wrong with these girls that a good whipping wouldn't sort out,' said the keeper, as he passed a scornful look over the girls in the room.

Edward scribbled more in his book as he glimpsed disapprovingly at the keeper.

'Not that we subscribe to such practices here....of course,' said the keeper.

A group of the girls quickly brushed the broken pottery to one side and picked up the sharp pieces by hand.

Edward strolled over to the keeper's desk and placed his hand over the large book of records. 'May I?' he said.

The keeper nodded.

Edward flipped open the book somewhere in the middle.

Tim peered over his shoulder. Name, date of apprehension, age....there were a good number of statistics here. Even the number of repeat visits.

Edward flipped through the pages, occasionally stopping to observe some numbers, jotting notes in his book.

'You're the keeper of the records, I presume?' said Edward.

The keeper nodded. 'Five years now sir.'

Edward continued to flip through the book.

'What do you reckon he's thinking about, Gemma. Look at his face. It's like he's trying to solve a puzzle.'

'Maybe the old man was right. Maybe he did know what Edward was looking for,' said Gemma.

When Edward had finished with the records, Gemma went to the keeper's log book. 'Tim, Tim, come here.'

'What is it?'

'Look. The entry here. It has to be today's entry. Or at least the most recent,' she said.

'So?'

'So, look at the year.'

Tim read it out, 'Sixteen ninety five.'

'We've gone back more than *three hundred* years.'

'What is it with this Spinning House then? I mean, why is Edward Noble here?'

'He's here because that old man outside suggested it to him,' she said.

'I know, but why did he listen?'

'I don't know,' said Tim. 'But remember when he was looking at the log book. The prison records?

Remember the look on his face. He's definitely found something in those records. It's like something clicked.'

'I know what you mean. Something caught his attention all right.'

As midnight fell on the Spinning House, Tim and Gemma wandered deeper into the corridors. Many of the inmates were already asleep in their beds.

'What's that noise?' said Gemma.

'I hear it too. Like a tapping noise. Seems to be coming from one of the windows.'

The tapping stopped.

'I think it was coming from this room,' said Tim as he opened the doors. Gemma followed him into the room.

Two young women stirred in their beds, half asleep. Thin cracks on the walls seemed to light up, as a faint noise floated over the girl's beds towards the window.

'Can you hear that hissing?' said Gemma. 'Like a....'

'Whisper,' said Tim.

One of the women sprang up in bed, eyes wide open and glanced at the window. She lit the candle by her bed and tiptoed over to the window.

'She looks frightened,' said Gemma.

The woman slowly spread her palms over the glass and whispered, 'I'm sorry......'

'Who's she talking to?' said Tim.

'No one. There's no one there.'

The window glazed over in a sheet of cloudy ice. The woman's breath visible as she exhaled in short gasps over the frosted pane. She tried to pull her hands away from the window, but struggled to move them.

'What's happening to her, Tim?'

Tim touched the glass and felt a dark, cold sensation take a grip of his body.

Gemma pulled him away. 'She's stuck Tim. She's stuck to the window.'

Tim turned as the room filled with the sound of whispers. The whispers were soft and unclear. Odd words stood out intermittently.

Gemma got as close to the window as she could without touching it, finding a small gap that hadn't frosted over.

'See anything?' said Tim.

'No, n...'

Crack.

A great big black bird smacked into the glass, right where Gemma was looking and made Gemma scream. She toppled backwards, looking for something to hold onto.

Tim grabbed her arm and they both turned to look at the bird perched on the window sill outside. Its gaze was fixed on the young woman, before turning to them with its coal coloured, soulless eyes.

'Tim, it can see us.'

'No, that's not possible.'

But just as Tim spoke, the bird turned to follow their movements.

'Come on, run,' said Gemma.

Tim was first to burst out of the room, with Gemma following. They whizzed past Edward Noble who was still talking to the keeper, and shot out of the front door.

Tim gripped a railing outside and skidded to one side. As he fell, Gemma tripped up and they both crumpled to the ground.

Tim was first to look up to the top of the building. A single, large black bird stared down at them and flapped its wings.

'It's coming Tim, quick help me up.'

Tim sprang to his feet and helped Gemma up. They were about to run when the old man appeared again.

Tim looked closer at the man's face. Those wrinkles. That rubbery face. The old man moved his hands together, forming the outline of a camera and made a noise like the closing of a shutter.

'It's you!' he said. 'You're the man in the TV!'

Gemma turned to Tim. 'He can't hear you.'

'The bird's coming. Run!'

As they sprinted down the street, the bird followed. It hovered some six feet from the ground and gained pace rapidly. Reaching the corner of the street, Gemma grabbed Tim's arm.

The book fell out of Tim's jacket pocket and he reached to the floor to pick it up. As he grabbed it, the pages flicked forward and stopped close to the last page. That's when everything started to blur.

'What's happening?' said Gemma. 'What did you do?'

Tim looked at the book. 'I just dropped the book,' he said, reaching to pick it up – observing the formulas on the open page.

'My legs, I can't feel them....it's happening again,' said Gemma.

Tim felt his head go all dizzy as the fuzzy image of a black bird coming towards him faded.

'Tim, I can't see anything,' said Gemma, as she clutched onto his arm.

Tim looked up as a bright light burst above them. Colours everywhere. Reds, yellows and blues danced on a bed of light a few inches from their heads. As the colours descended, Tim felt his whole body tingle and the background dissolve until everything went black.

CHAPTER FIFTEEN

Tim was first to open his eyes.

'Gemma, are you alright?'

'I think so. Where are we? I can hardly see a thing.'

Tim reached his arms out. 'I can feel a wall. Right here.' He continued to feel his way around the wall. 'We're in a small room.'

As he fumbled, he felt the cold touch of a metal door knob. 'Here it is.'

He turned the handle and opened the door. 'A corridor, come on let's go.'

Gemma opened a door on the left. Moonlight streamed through the large arched windows, casting a shadow over the chequered floor.

'Awesome!' said Gemma.

Tim glanced at Gemma, then up to the arched windows.

'Wren library. We're in Trinity College,' she said. 'Do you think we've come back to our own time?'

Tim looked around and shrugged. 'Look over there, Gemma, there's a light.'

'Careful, Tim, it's so dark in here.'

They strolled down the central passage of the library, trying not to knock over the large marble busts in the centre.

'It must be the middle of the night,' said Tim.

The light got closer, casting a long shadow on the wall below the arched windows.

'Is that who I think it is?' said Gemma.

Tim blinked. 'It can't be...'

Gemma nodded, 'it is, Tim, it's Edward Noble.'

'Yes, but look at him. He's...'

'Older. Much older. His hair's white!' she said.

'He must be, what...mid-forties? Fifty?'

'At least.'

'So we must be...,' Tim pondered for a moment. 'We must be somewhere between 1720 and 1730. Something like that.'

'We've gone forwards in time?'

Tim nodded. 'But how, all I did was drop the book?'

'You saw what happened. The book. It flipped open when you dropped it.'

'You think that's how we got here?'

Gemma nodded. 'As much as I don't want to believe it, it's like this book is helping us to travel in time.'

Sweat poured from Edward's face, his clothes covered in wood chippings and sawdust. Stood at a bookshelf, he positioned the last book on the second shelf, five places from the right hand side, turning some concealed wooden elements. He rubbed his hands together.

'Looks like he's done,' said Tim.

'So, he hid his *own* book in the library. That whole thing with the books on the second shelf. It was him,' said Gemma.

Edward brushed the wood shavings into a cloth sack and stopped for a moment. Like he was admiring the splendour of the library under the light of his candle. He put the candle down on the floor and appeared to hold his hands out on each side, as if he was holding hands. But there was no one there. He started to sing ever so quietly.

'Ring-a-ring of roses,
A pocketful of posies,
Attischo, Attischo,
We all fall down.'

He slumped to the ground, almost knocking his candle over with his foot. His face grim.

'What do you think *that* was all about?' said Gemma.

'No idea,' said Tim. 'Judging from these wood shavings, I'd say he's been here a few hours.'

'Do you think he's gone mad?' said Gemma.

'Well, he's definitely losing it. Singing nursery rhymes after midnight. Hiding secrets in a library.'

'Shhh,' said Gemma, 'what's that he's saying?'

'No one would believe me,' said Edward looking at the bookshelf, shaking his head as he ran his hands across the books on the shelf. 'It's too impossible.'

'What did he mean when he said no one would believe him?' said Gemma.

'He said "it's too impossible". Whatever he's written. He thinks...he thinks the world isn't ready to see it. He's afraid. That's why he's hiding it.'

'Hmmmm...,' said Gemma. 'So what's he written that's so important?'

Tim shrugged. 'Look, he's leaving.'

Gemma sighed.

'What's up with you?'

'Well, we know who he is. But not what he's written. We're none the wiser.'

'Yes, that's true. I still don't understand what it's all got to do with my mum. I mean how can it? All this happened centuries ago. It doesn't make any sense.'

'You're right, it doesn't make a lot of sense. But like you said, at least we know who wrote the book now,' she said.

'I think we need to get back to Trinity College,' said Tim. 'There must be someone who can make sense of his book. Someone who can make sense of those formulas.'

'A lecturer you mean?'

'Maybe a professor. We need to find the maths department and get some help.'

'Yes, Tim, you're right. But how? We're in the 1700's now and Edward Noble has only just hidden it. There's no chance anyone here is going to understand it. You heard what he said.'

'And we can't ask him, because he can't hear us.'

'We need to get back to our time,' she said. 'It's the only way we're going to get some answers. The only way to figure out how this links to your mum.'

'Your handbag, Gemma. We need the box. It has to be the way out of here. That's what brought us here in the first place.'

Gemma fished in her bag until she found the box. 'Here, take it,' she said. 'You really think it's going to take us back?'

'Let's hope so....Now, all I had to do last time was attach it to the compass, like this, and...' said Tim.

'Look, it's opening again, just like last time.'

Gemma grabbed onto his arm.

'Hold on Gemma....hold tight.'

Tim felt his body tingle and the background fade as bright colours surrounded them once more.

⇒⋅⇐

'Tim, look. It's taken us back, see,' said Gemma.

'You're right. There's the pond. We're back on the nature reserve,' said Tim, passing the box to Gemma.

Gemma nodded and put the box in her hand-bag. 'But it's daytime now. This time travel is very unpredictable. How's your head?'

'I still feel a bit dizzy, you?'

'The same. I never expected time travel would feel like this. It's like I've just had an operation or something. My feet are still tingling.'

'You're right, there's nothing cool about it, is there?'

Gemma tried to curl her toes. 'You still have the book?'

Tim patted his jacket, 'yes, it's here. Come on, Gemma. This book's at the heart of everything, it has to be. Whatever Edward Noble wrote. Well, it's the key to finding what happened to my mum. We've got to find help in Trinity College.'

'Can you remember the way?'

'I think so, follow me.'

CHAPTER SIXTEEN

Trinity College, Cambridge.

Tim and Gemma arrived at the small clearing in front of the Great Gate. A porter was giving directions to a group of Chinese tourists.

'Hello, I know this might seem a strange request, but could we possibly meet with one of the lecturers here? We've got a very important...project for school you see, and we'd like to see a maths lecturer if possible.'

'I'm sorry, Miss,' said the porter. 'The college is closed to visitors right now.'

Tim frowned, as one of the porter's colleagues came over.

'Actually, there's a free seminar starting in a few minutes. If you've got some questions, you could probably join it,' said the porter's colleague.

'Thanks, thanks a lot. Can we go through here?' said Gemma.

'Come on, follow me. You shouldn't really, but if I take you, it should be fine.'

As they passed through the gate, Tim took Gemma's arm. 'Gemma, look at this. Look at the size of this courtyard. It's even got a stone fountain, look.'

Inside the college, the porter lead them to a clearing where other students gathered for the seminar.

'Thanks for your help,' said Tim.

The porter nodded and went on his way.

'Now let's see if Edward Noble studied here and find someone who can explain this formula to us,' said Tim.

'You're not staying for the seminar?'

'No, of course not. Let's not waste time, Gemma. If I don't find out soon what's happened to Mum, I'm going to go mad.'

'Okay then. I'll see what I can find out about Edward Noble, you see if you can find a lecturer, okay?'

Tim nodded. 'We need to find a computer.'

'What about over there, look, isn't that a work area?'

Gemma sat down at one of the computers and began to search through details about past students.

As Tim studied a floor plan of the college pasted to a noticeboard he heard an authoritative voice from behind.

'Can I help you?' said Donald Hutchinson, a senior lecturer at the college.

Tim spun around on his chair and faced the lecturer. 'I'm looking for your most knowledgeable maths lecturer,' said Tim. 'Can you help?'

'You're in luck...,' said Donald, '..Laws. Professor Simon Laws is your man. I just passed him in the corridor.'

'Which way?' said Tim.

Donald pointed the way and Tim started to run.

Tim looked back, '..thanks...got to rush, sorry.'

Gemma turned to the lecturer. 'Don't worry about him. He's always in a rush.'

'The whole world is in a rush, Miss.'

She turned back to the university records, her finger tracing the names down the screen.

'Got you,' she squealed, as her fingers traced over the name. 'Edward Noble. You're my man.'

Grabbing her bag, she followed in quick pursuit of Tim. She caught him up, 'Edward Noble,' she said, panting.

'There he is!' said Tim.

'Edward Noble?'

'No..Simon Laws. He's our mathematician,' said Tim.

'I've found a match,' said Gemma, 'Edward Noble. The records show that he *was* a student here from 1694.'

'Mint! You were quick to find that,' said Tim. 'Well done you. Now all we have to do is figure out what his book is all about.'

They caught up with Professor Laws just as he was about to enter his den.

'Professor Laws?' said Tim.

'That'll be me,' said the professor.

'Can you spare us a few minutes of your time?' said Tim.

'I really am rather b....'

'Sorry, but this is important. We have something we want you to take a look at,' said Tim.

'Aren't you both a little too young to be...'

Tim opened the book and flicked through a couple of pages slowly.

Professor Laws raised his eyebrows on seeing a few snippets from the book. 'You better follow me... to my chambers.'

'To his *chambers*?' Tim whispered to Gemma, surprised that people still spoke that way in the twenty first century.

Once in the professor's den, Tim and Gemma sank into one of the softest and most luxurious sofas Tim had ever seen.

The professor reached out for the book with his skinny, wrinkly hand. 'May I?'

Tim let Professor Laws take the book.

'Where did you get this?'

Tim pondered for a moment, 'Oh. It's from a recent auction.'

'Really....?' said the professor. He put on his reading glasses and leant back into his stately brown leather chair. His facial expression said it all as each page he turned seemed to light him up more and more.

'Edward Noble,' said Gemma.

'Edward Noble?' said the professor.

'Yes, he was a student here.'

'One of mine?'

'A little before your time,' said Gemma.

The professor became more and more engrossed in the detail. He shot up, stepped away from the chair and darted over to the whiteboard on his wall. With the book in one hand and a marker pen in the other, he scribbled on the whiteboard.

'There's a reference here to a data source,' said the professor.

'A data source? Like records?' said Tim. 'There were some prison notes he made. Lots of names, dates and crimes.'

The professor put down the book, 'can I see?'

'We don't have them with us, I'm afraid.'

The professor frowned.

'But the one's we saw were from the Spinning House. Starting from 1695,' said Tim.

'The Spinning House?' said the professor.

'What *was* the Spinning House, Professor?' said Tim.

'It was a prison, of sorts.'

'Strange name for a prison,' said Gemma, winking at Tim.

'What does it all mean? All these notes. The formulas?' said Tim.

'Well, it has all the signs of a ... social study. Your Edward Noble had a thing for statistics you see.'

'Why prisons though?' said Gemma.

'Not prisons, strictly speaking. Back then, they were known as bridewells,' said the professor, 'Mr Noble, for whatever reason, found something in these statistics.'

'Bridewells! That's what the old man called it,' said Gemma.

Tim nodded, picked up the book and turned to what appeared to be the last page. 'Look, this is the last entry he made.'

The professor scanned the formula and scratched his head. He wiped the last equation off of his whiteboard and scribbled down the new formula. 'Remarkable....quite remarkable,' he said.

'How so?' said Gemma.

'I don't know whether to call it maths, or...'

'Or?' she said.

'Or..art.'

'Art?' said Tim. 'Why art?'

'Look at the drawings,' said the professor.

Gemma took the book and looked closer at some of the pencilled drawings in the margin, noticing the picture of the bird they had seen earlier.

'These look like some kind of scales,' she said. Gemma turned the page. 'What are those supposed to be?'

The professor studied the figures of people clumped together. 'Probably the plague. The plague of 1665,' he said, 'otherwise known as the Great Plague.'

'You can tell all that from the drawing?' said Gemma.

The professor turned the page and revealed another drawing, this time, with the year circled under the image of a dying man.

"1665."

The professor turned to the whiteboard. 'The formula though. It's not complete. Something is missing.'

'Missing?' said Tim.

'The last page. It was ripped out. In the library,' said Gemma, pointing to the perforated edge at the end of the book.

The professor scratched his head.

'What do you make of it all?' said Gemma, turning to the professor.

'I can't be sure. It's a ground breaking concept. But it must be a joke. Who's put you up to this?' The professor stomped over to the door and yanked it open, as if he was half expecting to see some of his colleagues lined up with their noses pressed against the door. He shook his head. 'You're familiar with radioactive decay theory?' he said, looking at Tim.

'Well, not in so many words..,' said Tim.

'Let me see, how can I put this,' said the professor, drumming his fingers on the arm of his brown leather chair. 'In a nutshell, it's not possible to predict when a given atom will decay. But if you take a sufficiently large sample of atoms, the chance that a given atom will decay is constant over time. It's governed by an exponential law you see.'

Tim turned to Gemma. His expression, blank.

The professor shot up, dashed to his whiteboard and plotted out a rough graph.

'Ah. One of those,' said Tim.

'What we have here, is a marriage, if you will, of probability theory and exponential law. Your Mr Noble was on the verge of defining...well...'

'Go on...defining?' said Gemma.

'Well, defining...social decay.'

'A formula..for social decay?' said Tim. 'Where's the sense in that?'

'Why would anyone want to make up a *formula* for that?' said Gemma.

The professor rubbed his chin. 'That I don't know. But what we have here is a man obsessed with finding an answer.'

'But social decay. What does that really *mean*?' said Tim.

'You have a lot of questions, don't you?' said the professor.

'If you knew what we'd been through these last few hours, you'd understand why.'

'Edward Noble clearly lived during a time when the quest for the truth was so strong, that men dedicated their lives in its pursuit,' said the professor. 'The *Age of Reason* they called it.' He rubbed his chin again and glanced at Gemma. 'You said he was a student here, from?'

Gemma paused for a moment, 'Oh...yes... from..16...err....94. Yes, that's it. 1694.'

The professor sprang up out of his chair and marched across the room to a beautifully crafted wooden bookcase, running his forefinger across several titles before stopping at a small reference book. He pulled the book from the shelf and skipped through the pages. 'Just as I thought. Did you know that Newton was Lucasian professor here at Cambridge between 1669 and 1702?'

'So...what does that prove?' said Tim.

'Lucasian professor of *mathematics*,' said the professor.

'Are you suggesting that Edward Noble might have known Newton?' said Gemma.

'Quite possible,' said the professor.

'What's this Lucasian professor thing anyway?' said Tim.

'Well, perhaps one of the most famous academic chairs in the world,' said the professor. 'You've heard of Stephen Hawking? He used to be the Lucasian professor here, in this college.'

Gemma nodded. 'Everyone's heard of Stephen Hawking. He's a genius!'

'You said the formula isn't complete?' said Tim, recalling what the professor had said earlier.

'I said *something* is missing,' said the professor.

'Same thing.'

'No, sir, it's not.'

'So what's missing?' said Tim.

'It's his proof isn't it. The proof of his theory?' said Gemma.

The professor nodded. 'Top marks, Miss...?'

'It's Gemma, just Gemma.'

'You see, his notes have a few workings in them. But the formal proof, it's not here.'

'The bird in the library,' whispered Tim.

Gemma nodded.

Tim stared at the whiteboard and focussed on the formula.

'Is it just me, or has it just got colder in here?' said Gemma.

'Look!' said Tim, 'the window!'

'What the....,' said the professor.

'Quick, Professor, move away from the window,' said Gemma.

Two large hands appeared under the window and lifted it up.

'Daniel!' shouted Tim.

Daniel stepped down from the window and strode over to Gemma.

'See what your stupid cat did?' said Daniel, showing her the deep cut down the left side of his face.

Tim recalled the struggle they had earlier when the bird tried to take his compass.

'Who the devil are you?' said the professor.

'Never you mind, Simon,' said Daniel, wiping the text from the whiteboard with his hand. He stared at Gemma and licked his hand from top to bottom, until his tongue was black.

'How do you know my n...?' said the professor.

'Name? Ah yes, let's just call it my party trick, shall we?'

'What do you want?' said Tim.

Daniel ignored the question and surveyed the room. 'Where is it? Where's the book?'

Gemma had the book behind her back and passed it to Tim.

A faint whisper came from the window. Daniel smiled, strode over to Tim and reached behind his back. 'I'll take that,' said Daniel. He grabbed the book from Tim, jumped onto the leather chair and leapt out of the window.

The professor ran to the phone on his desk and called security, giving them a description of Daniel and a warning to proceed with caution.

Crackle.

'What was that *noise*?' said the professor.

Tim glanced at Gemma. 'No time to explain,' he said, 'run!'

As they sprinted to the door, the window frosted over in a sheet of ice. A loud crash emanated around the room as a dozen large, black birds smashed through the window – ice flying around the room, shattering into tiny pieces.

Tim turned back momentarily. The birds pecked at the whiteboard and danced around the whole room – their wings sending loose papers into the air, as others dived into them and pecked the paper into pieces. Tiny morsels of paper showered the room, covering the sofa and leather chair.

A whisper from the window called the birds away and they formed a line as they darted out – bits of paper caught up in their wings. As the last bird flew out, the shattered ice rose from the floor and sprayed itself over the open space in the window, first forming a frost, then turning back to glass.

It was as if the glass had never shattered.

Tim slammed the door shut and darted after Gemma and the professor, sprinting down the corridor. Their fiery paced steps echoed noisily around the college walls.

The professor slowed down as he turned a corner. 'Wait. I have to catch my breath.'

'Which way now?' said Gemma.

'Down here,' said the professor. 'We've got to get to the Master's Lodge and raise the alarm.'

Tim turned to the windows and looked out onto the large courtyard – the Great Court as it was known locally – the largest courtyard in the college. In the centre of the courtyard he could just make out Daniel stood by the ornate stone fountain, with its impressive archways.

'Gemma, I see Daniel, he's got the book. We have to get it back.'

Gemma and Tim stopped running and both looked out of one of the hall's windows.

'What's Daniel doing?' said Gemma. 'Who's that with him?'

Tim looked again and saw Daniel with another man. A much younger man. 'We've got to get closer, come on.'

'Hey, where's the professor?' said Gemma.

'He's down there look. He said he wanted to raise the alarm. Come on, there's a way out over there.'

Tim pushed Gemma's head down as they came out of the building onto the courtyard. He got on his hands and knees and crawled on the ground. 'Come on, otherwise they'll see us.'

Tim led the way, close to the wall of the building.

'This must be the Master's Lodge, where the professor was heading,' said Gemma, looking up to her side. 'Ouch. I just caught myself on the ivy. Look, it's all over the walls.'

'If we can make it over there, we can probably get to the fountain without them seeing us. If we keep down.' Tim turned to his right and brushed against the Chapel, crawling like a mouse. He turned to the fountain and squinted as the sunshine hit him. He could just make out Daniel's outline.

'Look who it is. With Daniel,' said Gemma. 'It's the Goth.'

'Daniel's giving him the book. Come on, let's keep going.'

As Tim approached the fountain, Daniel swaggered towards the Great Gate, opposite the Master's Lodge on the other side of the courtyard. Tim could see Goth Boy put the book inside his black leather jacket. He jumped on Goth Boy's back and pulled him to the ground. As they scuffled Gemma pounced onto Goth Boys legs and pinned him down.

'Got it,' said Tim, as he reached inside Goth Boy's leather jacket and pulled out the book.

'I don't think so,' said Daniel, as he spun around and looked straight at Tim.

'What's he doing?' said Gemma.

'I'm not sure,' said Tim.

'Come on, my children,' said Daniel, outstretching his arms, looking up at the Chapel rooftop.

'Look!' said Gemma.

An army of birds sprang up from the castle-like turrets that lined the Chapel's rooftop. Spaced equidistant between the turrets were taller, pointed stone turrets – each with a bird perched on them. There must have been some twelve or so pointed turrets.

On a nod from Daniel, about a dozen birds plunged down over the courtyard and landed on his outstretched arms. Tiny bits of shredded paper fell from their wings onto his coat like snowflakes on a cold winter's day.

'Look how the birds are flocking around him,' said Gemma.

Tim nodded. 'He must be their leader.'

Tim heard a loud squawk from above and looked towards the Great Gate. A large bird, sat between two castle-like turrets on the Great Gate, jerked its head towards the fountain in the centre of the courtyard, then to Tim.

'What's he doing?' said Gemma, as Daniel raised his arms higher.

Tim felt a pain in his ribs as Goth Boy kicked him, forcing Gemma to press down harder on Goth Boy's legs.

'Give me the book, Tim-o-thee', said Daniel, looking at the birds on each of his arms.

The bird above the Great Gate swooped down to the courtyard below and landed with a thud on the grassy turf near the Chapel, stumbling for a second before regaining its footing. Then it began to walk closer to Tim.

'I'm not going to ask you again. Give..me..the.. book,' said Daniel as one of the birds on Daniel's arms flapped its wings.

'All this for a formula about social decay?' said Tim. He pulled Goth Boys arms closer to his chest.

Tim could see Daniel grit his teeth.

'Ouch!' screamed Tim, as the bird pecked his leg. He kicked the bird away with his shoe, sending it tumbling along the grass.

'Your miserable existence is coming to an end,' said Daniel. 'For all of you. You really think we're about to stand by and watch you undo all the work we've done. Centuries of work.'

Tim glanced at Gemma. 'What is it Gemma, what's wrong?'

'It's them. The social decay, they're behind it. The Deceivers. Don't you see Tim. Everything they do. They're trying to...'

'Trying to what, Gemma?'

'Trying to destroy all the goodness in the world. That's what this is about isn't it?' said Gemma looking at Daniel.

'Well done. You've just graduated to the top of the class.'

'But why? How is that even possible?' said Tim.

Daniel gritted his teeth again. 'A whisper here, a whisper there,' then he laughed. 'You're such a weak race. So feeble. So...suggestible.'

Gemma turned to Daniel, 'so you're afraid of anyone getting the book. Understanding the formula. You're afraid people will wake up? Reverse social decay?'

Daniel lashed out at Gemma with his claws, cutting the straps on her handbag, forcing it to the ground.

'These days we have so little to do. Your kind have become so good at it. Jack the Ripper. World War Two. Global Warming. You're *so* much better at it than we are. Such imagination. We're just giving you a helping hand, that's all.'

'And my mum, what's this got to do with her?'

'Your mum-my got in the way,' said Daniel.

'What did she ever do to you?' said Tim.

'You really don't know do you?'

Tim shook his head.

'Your mother has a gift, Tim-o-thee. A gift that we simply cannot allow.'

'Has? What do you mean? You said she was dead.'

'Oops...,' said Daniel, putting his hand over his mouth.

'He's a Deceiver, Tim. You can't believe anything he says,' said Gemma, quickly tying the broken straps of her handbag together.

'But don't worry, Tim-o-thee, you'll never find her. Not ever.'

'Where is she?' shouted Tim. He felt his temples throb. His heartbeat quicken. His cheeks flush.

'Somewhere you'll never find her.' He waved his arms, released the birds into the air and watched as they circled the fountain. Their wings extended. As the birds came closer to each other, their wings locked together. Darkness engulfed the Great Court. Blackness surrounded Tim and Gemma, shadowing the entire courtyard.

It felt like day had become night.

Goth Boy kicked Tim, pushed him over and forced the compass to fall out of his pocket. As the compass tumbled across the courtyard its lid opened and a blue glow shot upwards towards the black sky.

Daniel stepped back from Tim and Gemma, covering his eyes, moving away from the beam of light coming out of the compass. Goth Boy sprinted to Daniel's side, looking away from the light.

'Look what the light's doing to the birds,' said Gemma, as the birds shook their wings uncomfortably.

'They're breaking up, Gemma, look!' said Tim.

'They're falling out of the sky!' she said.

'Get him!' shouted Daniel, eyes covered as he pointed towards Tim.

A group of birds rose up high above the Chapel, avoiding the main beam of light from the compass and descended towards the centre of the courtyard where Tim was crouched.

Daniel's eyes narrowed and he turned to the fountain. He started to sprint, raised his arms in the air and jumped. 'Get the compass!' he shouted.

Goth Boy dived onto the ground and spread his fingers out, trying to avoid the light from the compass, burning one of his nails. He pulled his hand back, then grabbed it quickly, pushing the lid down and stopping the light.

'Tim, it's the Goth. He's got the compass,' said Gemma.

The Goth smiled and curled his fingers around the compass. He turned to face the fountain, smiled at Tim, then threw the compass into the stone base.

'No!' shouted Tim.

Tim sprinted to the fountain and picked up the compass, noticing its cover had been dented.

'Tim, look. Daniel...he's....he's changing...,' said Gemma as Daniel transformed into a large black bird and took flight above the fountain.

'No such thing as monsters?' said Tim, putting the compass back in his pocket.

Gemma stared back at him, her mouth wide open.

Daniel's bird-like form swooped over the fountain and charged towards Tim, narrowly missing him.

'Not him too!' said Gemma, as Goth Boy's arms became wings.

'Quick, that way!' said Tim.

As Daniel shot up above the fountain, more birds descended – the first just inches from Gemma's head.

Daniel dived from the structure above the fountain towards Tim.

Tim couldn't help feel that it was all over. This is where it would end. The birds would have his eyes. Just as Goth Boy's painting had predicted.

'Compass!' said Gemma, 'try the compass again. It worked last time.'

'I don't know Gemma, it's been badly damaged.'

'Come on, what choice do we have...quick, they're coming.'

'Okay,' said Tim, scrambling to find the compass in his pocket. He pulled it out as one of the birds was about to snatch it and filled the courtyard with a bright blue glow.

The light hit the bird-like forms of Daniel and Goth Boy and forced them to transform back to human form. Daniel fell to the grass below and curled up in a ball. Goth Boy hit the top of the ornate structure on top of the fountain and tumbled to the ground, grazing his head against the stone.

Birds flew out of control and fell out of the sky.

Tim felt a sharp pain, like he'd just been stung by a giant bumble bee. Blood gushed out in short spurts. He passed the compass to Gemma, clasped his arm and let out a cry that filled the courtyard.

The tip of the bird's beak was red. Covered in his blood. As it the hit the ground, Gemma kicked it hard, smashing it against the base of the fountain, feathers flying in the air.

'Tim, your hurt!' said Gemma.

Tim applied more pressure on the cut, trying to stop the blood.

'What's happening, Tim, the compass....something's wrong,' said Gemma, trying to shake the compass as the blue light flashed intermittently.

Gemma turned to Tim and froze.

'It's broken,' said Tim, taking the compass off Gemma. 'Must have been the fountain,' he said, as the light stopped glowing.

Daniel crawled along the grass on the other side of the fountain and pushed himself up on his feet. He looked up as another wave of birds rose above the Chapel. There were hundreds of them in the sky, flying in a series of random circles. They bumped into each other, one after another – and the sky around them darkened. It was as if they were creating rain clouds. Each time they bashed into one another, more rain clouds were formed. As the sky darkened further, thunder echoed around the courtyard, followed by zigzag flashes of lightning. Heavy rain poured down, spraying Tim moments before he and Gemma took cover under Queen Gate's archway.

Daniel marched fearlessly towards Tim, clenching his fists as he approached Queen's Gate.

Tim looked up. He turned towards Daniel, with no more than fifteen feet between them.

Another lightning flash lit up the fountain. Thunder roared around the courtyard in a series of small explosions. A thunderbolt struck one of the Chapel's windows, shattering the glass into small pieces.

'Hold it tight,' said Gemma, taking a handkerchief from her bag and wrapping it around Tim's wound.

'Look!' shouted Tim.

Daniel held his hand out to Goth Boy and helped him to his feet.

'They're getting closer. What shall we do?' said Gemma.

Sirens sounded.

'Did you hear that?' said Tim.

'Yes, look over there, it's the professor,' she said.

'He's got some security with him, look,' said Tim.

'Those are police sirens. Look over there, on the other side – the police are coming onto the courtyard,' she said.

The courtyard became a hive of activity as police swarmed the area.

The professor ran over to Queen's Gate, where Tim and Gemma were taking cover, holding a newspaper over his head.

'You two, are you alright?'

'Watch out!' shouted Tim, 'behind you!'

Daniel outstretched his claws and lashed out at the professor, shredding the newspaper above his head.

'What the..?' said the professor.

Two security guards, lagging behind the professor, came up behind Daniel and tried to force him to the ground. As one of them pulled at Daniel's arm, Goth Boy struck him over the head and knocked him to the ground.

The police charged up the side of the building from the Master's Lodge, and spread out in a rough line – two of the officers dived at Goth Boy's legs and forced him down.

Daniel was just a few feet away from Tim and Gemma when one of the police officers pulled out his truncheon and struck Daniel on the back of the neck. Daniel spun around and grabbed the truncheon with his claws, breaking it in two. The police officer stepped backwards, his face turning a ghostly white as Daniel started to chew on one of the truncheon pieces.

'What are you?' said the police officer.

Daniel smirked. 'I'm your worst nightmare,' he said, pushing the officer to the ground.

Another four police officers pounced on Daniel and forced him to the ground. One officer was able to clip the cuffs on his wrists, avoiding his sharp claws. Daniel struggled and looked towards Queen's Gate, just as the professor blocked his view.

Daniel glanced at the police officers around him and raised his arms in the air.

'What's he doing?' said one of the officers.

'Christ!' said the other officer. 'Look. He's changing. Into a.... bird'. The police officers jumped up and looked at each other as the bird flew low and dived at the officers who'd grounded Goth Boy. Daniel's bird-like form knocked the officers down with its huge wing span.

Tim turned to Gemma, 'look, the Goth, he's changing too.'

'What was that?' said the professor, turning as the Goth took flight over the officers' heads.

'They're all over the place,' said Tim. All around the courtyard birds attacked the police as they tried to hold them back with their truncheons.

'More police,' said Gemma, pointing over at the Great Gate. Soon the courtyard was full of forty or so officers and medical staff.

Stunned birds were littered all over the courtyard. Paramedics were attending to wounded officers - cuts and bruises to their arms and legs. The base of the fountain covered in blood.

As the bird-like forms of Daniel and Goth Boy rose high above the Great Gate, the remaining birds followed them in formation and flew beyond the college, towards Bridge Street.

'They're getting away,' said Tim.

'Never mind that, are you alright my boy?' said the professor.

Tim nodded.

'Can we get a paramedic over here?' said the professor. One of the police officers nodded and spoke on his walkie-talkie.

'No...really...it's not necessary, it's just a graze,' said Tim.

'Come on Tim, you should have it looked at. What if you need a tetanus jab or something?' said Gemma.

Tim shrugged and glanced at his wound.

'Just what are those....things, anyway?' said the professor.

Gemma looked at the professor, her face solemn. 'Deceivers, Professor.'

'Deceivers, you say?'

'Yes, that's what they call themselves.'

'I've never seen anything like it,' said the professor.

Tim pulled the book out of his jacket pocket. 'Daniel, their leader, he was after this.'

The professor nodded. 'I could see that. But why? All this, for a book?' he said, looking around the courtyard at the casualties.

'It's not just a book. As you said yourself. It's got a formula that defines social decay.'

'Yes, yes, my boy, but that's just academic.'

'No,' said Gemma. 'That's just it, it's not just academic. Not for them. They believe that they can destroy goodness.'

'Destroy goodness? Whatever do you mean, Miss?'

'I mean, see social decay through to its logical end - until there's no goodness left in the world.

That's why they want the book. They want to stop us from figuring it out. From healing ourselves.'

'Us?'

'Yes, the human race. You saw yourself. They're not human.'

'And you believe this nonsense too?' said the professor, turning to Tim.

Tim nodded. 'It's not nonsense, Professor. We've seen what these Deceivers can do. It's like Daniel said, a whisper here, a whisper there. They prey on the weak. A suggestion. A thought.'

'But why?' said the professor.

'Because they can. I don't know. That's their thing.'

'Monsters...in the real world? I just can't believe it.'

'You saw it with your own eyes, Professor. Believe it.'

One of the police officers called the professor over. 'Please excuse me,' said the professor.

Gemma put her hand gently on the handkerchief that covered Tim's wound. 'I bet it's killing you, isn't it?'

Tim smirked, 'I hope not!'

In the distance Tim could make out a police photographer taking pictures of the courtyard. It looked like a number of birds were dead, but thankfully no people. Plenty of policemen were injured though.

'You look puzzled,' said Gemma.

'I was just thinking,' said Tim, as the police photographer snapped his shutter. 'Remember when I said the old man outside the Spinning House was the same man I saw in the TV set?'

Gemma nodded.

'What if *he's* the postman? You saw what he did outside the Spinning House. The old man. He pretended to take a photo. Don't you remember? Just like the postman did in the coffee shop and the old man in the TV.'

'Come on, I told you earlier that the postman was probably your man in the TV. '

'I couldn't see it then. I don't understand how, but he must have been in disguise. It makes sense. If the postman really is Daniel's enemy. If he really sent the compass. That store, where I got the kaleidoscope. It was the first place I found with the compass. What if it's not a coincidence? You said yourself that the kaleidoscope may have been a way to show me how my paintings make people feel.'

Gemma shrugged.

'You really think I have a gift?' he said.

'I know what I felt when I saw your painting. That was real. It wasn't like anything I've felt before. So yes, I think you've got a gift. I don't know what it means though.'

'Tell me again how it made you feel.'

'Hard to explain really. You know how you get butterflies in your stomach when you're excited. It was a bit like that. Like I said before, it was a warm feeling. I felt positive. Confident. It felt good.'

Tim slapped his head. 'That's it, Gemma, that's what's been bothering me.'

'What?'

'It's all connected. It must be. The dream, my painting, the book, the Deceivers. It's what the Professor said, you know, about social decay.'

'I'm not following you, Tim.'

'If this formula about social decay is right, then all goodness is going to end, yes?'

'Yes. Maybe. I don't know.'

'What if my gift can stop it, or slow it down?'

'Stop it?'

'Yes, you just said it yourself. You said my painting made you "feel good". What if that's my gift? What if it has the opposite effect on them.'

'Well, I remember the Goth ran out of the art club when he saw your painting. He didn't look too happy. Like he was in pain.'

'Yes, it makes sense doesn't it?'

Gemma nodded. 'Maybe a long shot.'

'Gemma, I think we should get out of here before the police come and ask us for a statement.'

Tim led the way out of the Queen's Gate.

A short while later they sat down on a bench by the River Cam, looking over at the punts, with Wren Library stood proudly ahead of the river.

In the distance Tim could make out a lone figure walking across the grass towards him.

'Daniel!' shrieked Gemma.

'And look, he's on his own.'

Daniel stopped a few steps away from the bench and lit a cigarette.

Tim reached in his pocket. 'You've seen what the compass can do, not one more step,' he said.

'I'm not going to ask you again. Give me the book,' said Daniel.

'I'm not joking, I'll open it,' said Tim, pressing his finger lightly on the button.

Daniel took a step back.

'Your compass is broken,' said Daniel, pointing to the dent on the cover.

'Are you prepared to take that chance?' said Tim. 'You want the book and I want my mum back, right?'

Daniel snarled.

Tim turned to Gemma, then to Daniel. 'So, let's do a trade.'

'A trade?' said Daniel, looking nervously at the compass.

'Yes, my mum for the book.'

Daniel sighed, looking at the compass. 'Very well. Meet me at the Ever-gale forest,' and with that, Daniel turned and took flight.

'Hang on, where exactly?'

'It's too late, Tim, he's gone.'

Tim plugged "Evergale forest" into his mobile phone and a map came up.

'Come on, Gemma, let's go.'

'You think we can trust him?'

'No, Gemma, I don't think we can trust him one bit.'

'But it's not safe. We can't meet him alone. We need help.'

'Gemma, the last thing we want now is the police asking us lots of questions. They're not going to believe us anyway. Remember how you felt when I first told you about the birds. The man in the TV?'

'But it's not the same now. The Professor. The police. They've seen with their own eyes.'

'They've only seen a fraction. Look, Gemma, this is my only chance to find mum. If she's really alive, this is the only way. We've got the compass. You've seen what it does to them, that's our safety net. You know, if there's any trouble.'

'But you saw what happened. The light. It stopped. What if it's really broken?'

'I have to believe it, Gemma. There's no choice.'

Gemma sighed. 'I don't know why I listen to you.'

CHAPTER SEVENTEEN

Tim switched off his mobile.

'I can't get any reception. We're too far out. But this is the forest,' said Tim.

'I've never even heard of this forest. Evergale you said?'

Tim nodded.

'It looks huge. We don't even know where to meet him. Look at all these trees. What if they've set traps. It's just not safe, Tim.'

'You have a better idea?'

Gemma shrugged. 'Which way now, then?' she said.

Tim turned from side to side, sighed and pulled out the compass.

'It's still not glowing is it?' she said.

Tim looked at the compass. 'No, the only thing it's doing...is pointing north. So come on, let's head north.'

'Do you really think you're going to find your mum? In here? You really believe Daniel's going to give her up?'

'He wants the book doesn't he? Come on, let's keep going.'

'It's going to be getting dark soon. I hope you're right about this.'

An hour passed and still nothing.

'I'll have to stop for a minute, Tim. My feet are killing me.'

Gemma sat on a fallen tree trunk and took off one of her shoes, shaking the small leaves out from inside, turning to massage her foot.

'That's better,' she said.

Tim sat beside her and rested his chin on his hands.

'What are you thinking, Tim?'

'What could the Deceivers want with my mum?'

'I don't know. Daniel said she had a gift. Something they couldn't allow. They must have taken her. You know, because of the gift.'

'What I still can't understand is how my painting made that map that lead us to the library. You know, Wren library. If that hadn't happened we'd have never found the book in the first place.'

'What if that's *your* gift, Tim?'

'My gift? What, hiding stuff in paintings? Hardly sounds like a gift does it. Especially when I didn't really find it. You did!'

Tim sighed and raised the compass in the air. 'Is your foot okay?'

Gemma nodded, ' I think so, it just hurts a bit.'

'Come on, let's carry on.'

'Look Tim, a field, over there.'

As they rose above a small mound of earth, Tim pointed. 'Not just a field. Look Gemma. A lake.'

As they approached a thick oak tree, there was another opening in the forest, beyond the tree, some hundred metres away.

'What's that over there?' said Gemma.

'Looks like some kind of adventure playground. There's a building in the middle of it look. Like a big wooden shed. Tread carefully, Gemma. Just in case.'

'I can't see anyone around, Tim,' said Gemma. 'It looks deserted. Are you sure this is the right place? What was that?'

'I heard it too, it came from over there, by those trees,' said Tim.

Tim looked up. A faint flash of red light – like a ribbon, rushed past his eyes, high up in the trees. 'I'm not sure. Not sure what I saw.'

'We're almost at the building. Let's get down, just in case they see us.'

They crouched level with the base of the building. It was a simple rectangular building, made of dark wood. The windows were frosted over, so there was no way to see inside.

'Let's check it out,' said Tim.

'Yes, but how?'

Tim put his ear against one of the wooden walls and listened. 'I can't hear a thing inside. Maybe it's empty?'

'It's creepy here. The whole place looks run down. What's that frame over there for?'

'Maybe it's one of those outdoor adventure parks.'

'So where's the advertising board? Where's the name?'

'You've got a point.'

They crawled along the base of the building and turned the corner.

'Look, a door,' said Gemma.

'I still can't see anyone. Not even a bird. Come on, let's get up.'

Gemma was first to reach the door. 'Shall I?' she said, her hand primed to turn the wooden knob.

Tim looked behind, then back to the door. 'Yes, do it.'

Gemma turned the handle. 'It's. It's open.'

'That's strange,' whispered Tim, as he pushed the door open. 'It's like a proper house in here. Look at the walls.'

'Yes, they're all rendered. It's so white in here.'

The inside was on one level and its spacious entrance lead to two rooms with white panelled doors.

'Feels like a clinic,' said Gemma.

'Smells like a hospital,' he said.

'You *still* think it's an adventure playground?'

Tim shrugged.

'What do you think those poles are for? Sticking out of the walls up there?'

'A bit too high for coat hangers aren't they.'

'It feels warm doesn't it? But I can't see any radiators.'

Tim pressed his hands against the brilliant white walls and dragged his hands across until they fell flush with the panelled door to the right.

'No door handle,' said Tim.

'So how do we get in?'

'We look for a key.'

'Hey, what's that up there, above the door?'

'Another pole?'

'No, just above the pole to the right. There's a small hole there. What do you think it is?'

'It looks too thin to be a keyhole. Give me your hands, I need a leg up. If I can just hold on to the top of the frame I think I can reach the pole.'

Gemma gave Tim a leg up and he stretched, his fingers just an inch away from the white pole.

'I can't hold you much longer. Can you reach it?' said Gemma.

'Al-most...Yes, there.'

Tim hung onto the short pole and reached his right hand towards the slit above the door. He tried to push his finger inside, but it was too thick.

'I need something thinner.' He thought for a moment. 'Wait. House key.' He switched hands and tried to hold his balance with his right hand while digging in his left pocket for his house key. He pressed the key into his right hand and switched to hang from his left.

Gemma skipped over to the entrance door and poked her head outside.

'Anything?' said Tim.

'All clear,' said Gemma.

Tim pushed the tip of the key into the slit and felt it hit a spongy mechanism as it almost sucked the head of the key in. He pulled back on the key and fell to the ground.

'What's that noise?' said Gemma, as the door buzzed.

The buzz stopped and was followed by a loud click. The door opened a few inches.

Tim didn't move.

'Why aren't you going in?' said Gemma.

'Can you hear that? Scratching. It's coming from inside.' He put his finger to his lips and turned to Gemma.

Gemma nodded.

He made small steps, treading very quietly. His mind wandered to thoughts of the quiet slippers the old man had in the library. That's just what he needed right now.

The room was full of colour and very large. It must have been at least thirty metres square. A bed, a chair.

But who was that?

Sat at a small table by the window to the right, was a lone figure scribbling on paper.

The figure didn't turn.

Gemma followed Tim into the room and raised her eyebrows as she saw the colourful images on the wall, before fixing her attention on the lone figure by the table.

Tim struggled to find the words.

He took two more quiet steps forward.

His first attempt was barely more than a whisper, 'Mum...?'

He took another step towards the figure.

'Mum, is that *you*?'

The figure, clearly the frame of a woman in her mid-thirties, stopped scribbling on the paper and froze.

Tim felt himself choking up as the woman turned. His eyes moist. As the woman turned to face him, an image of the photo on his bedside cabinet flashed into his mind.

The woman put her hands on her head and dropped what looked like a pencil to the floor. She stepped to the side of the chair, took a step forwards and reached out her arms.

'Timothy? Tim! Is that you?'

She took a hold of his arms at first. 'Is that *really* you?'

He felt the lump in his throat was going to explode. 'Yes...yes Mum, it's me. I can't believe it,' said Tim. 'I can't believe we found you.'

It was like time had stopped. All those police interviews. The warnings to expect the worst. Was the nightmare finally over?

He could smell peaches. That smell. It really was his mum.

'I don't know what to say,' said Tim. He plunged his arms around his mum's waist. 'We thought you'd....'

Tim held his mum tightly. His head filled with all the things they had to catch up on.

'Just look at you...,' said his mum. She ran her fingers through his wavy hair. 'My beautiful boy. I'm so proud of you.'

Wiping the tears from her eyes, Tim's mum stood back slightly and took his hands into hers, gripping tightly. 'Tim. How did you find me? How did you get in here? It's heavily guarded. It's not safe.'

'But Mum, we didn't see anyone. It's like it's deserted.'

Gemma surveyed the room. Crooked wooden pots with homemade paint littering the table. Images on the walls. Birds. The forest. It was incredible. This is how Tim's mum had spent the last year. Alone in this room.

Gemma went to the window. 'Hey, I can see outside.' She saw the forest and what looked like a swing, close the the climbing frame. 'It's so quiet in here,' said Gemma. 'I can't hear the forest at all.' She turned to the door. 'And that door, it's so *thick*.' She moved closer and touched the material on the side of the door. 'It's soft in the middle, but it feels like. Material?'

Tim's mum nodded. 'Yes. It's sound proof you see. Nothing gets in. Nothing gets out.' She hurried over to the window and scanned the forest. 'I don't understand.'

'Mum?'

'The birds. They're normally everywhere. Look Tim, it's not safe here. If they find you here, I don't know what they'll do. You didn't answer my question. How did you find me?'

'We offered Daniel a trade. This book for you,' said Tim, showing the book to his mum.

His mum turned to the book, a puzzled look on her face.

'Mum, we have to get you out of here. You're coming back with us.'

His mum fell to her knees and pressed her hands to her face. She turned from wall to wall, looking at the images.

'Mum?'

'I just can't believe this is really happening,' she said. 'It's been so long.'

'A year, Mum.'

'A year!'

'Yes, Mum. I can't believe you're alive.'

'And Dad? He's...he's okay?'

'Yes, Mum, he's just fine. Wait till he sees you. He's not going to believe it.'

'Come on Tim. I have a bad feeling about this,' said Gemma, looking out the window.

'Mum. We have to go.'

His mum pressed her hands against the paintings on the wall and appeared to caress them. 'Wait, I have to take my things.' She scurried to the table where she'd been scribbling and picked up a wad of papers. Papers full of writing and sketches. Folding them, she glanced at Gemma and then at Gemma's handbag. 'Could you?'

Gemma obliged, curled them up so they'd fit in her bag and followed Tim and his mum out of the room. Once out of the room, Tim's mum looked up at one of the poles in the entrance area.

'Mum, what's wrong.'

'They're not here.'

'What's not here?' said Gemma.

Tim's mum turned to the pole. 'The birds. They're always there. On the poles.'

'I really don't like the look of this,' said Gemma.

Cautiously, all three of them peered around the entrance door, to the waiting forest.

A loud insect noise started up.

'What was that?' said Tim, as a stream of green and brown ribbons flashed across the forest, before fading away. 'Did you see *that*!'

'No Tim, I don't see anything,' said his mum.

'I can hear that sound though,' said Gemma. 'Some kind of animal? Insect?'

'I've heard that before...,' said his mum.

'But how could you. You know, from in there,' said Tim, nodding his head back to the room they'd just left.

'They let me out. You know, for air. Exercise. Twice a day. Once in the morning and once in the early evening. It's the first time I've been able to talk freely outside though. It feels good.'

'This way?' said Gemma, pointing to the climbing frame to their left.

Tim nodded.

'You look uneasy?' said Gemma.

'It's these noises,' said Tim. 'The insects probably. Getter louder. I keep seeing colours everywhere.' Green and brown colours flashed by his eyes again. Brighter this time.

All three of them spun around and turned to their right as a loud clap beat out, slowly at first.

'Bravo!' came a voice.

Gemma spun to the left, looking beyond the climbing frame.

'Very well done!' came a voice, this time from a different direction.

The clapping got louder.

A branch cracked and Tim saw a flash of black streaming across his field of vision in a wave of ribbons.

Tim blinked.

'You!' shouted Tim, now face to face with Daniel, who was grinning broadly.

'Who's a *clever* boy then,' said Daniel.

Tim's mum clasped Tim's arm for comfort and turned away from Daniel's face.

'Do you really think we'd make it so easy for you? Do you really think we are so stupid?' Picking up a branch, he held both ends and violently snapped it in two. He turned his head most unnaturally, almost a hundred degrees and stared straight at Gemma. 'Now. You. You have something that belongs to me.' He glanced at her handbag.

'Don't give it to him, Gemma,' said Tim.

'Don't give it to him, Gem-ma,' said Daniel in a squeaky voice.

Tim's mum stood back, filled her lungs and was about to open her mouth when a pair of hands clasped her mouth from behind.

Gemma screamed as Goth Boy appeared behind Tim's mum and tied a long stem of a plant around her mouth.

'Not a word,' said Goth Boy, putting his finger to his lips as he stared at Tim's mum.

Goth Boy yanked Tim's mum's arms behind her back and held them tightly. 'Shhhhhh now,' he said.

Daniel marched over to Tim.

'Is this where you were cut?' asked Daniel, holding out Tim's wounded arm. He pulled the wounded area closer to his face, stuck out his tongue and tasted the wound, wincing as if he'd just swallowed a lemon. 'I'm not going to ask you again,' he said, frowning at Gemma.

Tim turned to Gemma and violently shook his head.

Gemma reached in her bag, pulled out the book and thrust it in Daniel's hands. 'Here! Choke on it!'

'Such gusto. Such *passion* my dear. Why, with passion like that, you should. You should. Teach art!' He laughed violently.

Goth Boy laughed with him, before turning to Tim's mum and licking the beads of sweat from her neck.

Tim's mum flinched and tried to free herself from his grip.

Gemma turned to Goth Boy. 'You monster.'

'I didn't think you believed in monsters,' said Goth Boy.

Gemma turned away.

Goth Boy blew an empty kiss and turned to Tim's mum. 'What should I do with her?'

'Oh, that's easy, she goes back in there,' said Daniel, nodding at the wooden hut.

'We had a deal,' said Tim. 'A trade. The book for my mum, remember?'

'A trade. No, there's going to be no trade here. I have the book. I have your mum. All's well with the world.' He paused. 'Wait, I take that back. Of course, all's not well with the world thanks to you. Now I've got the book, you haven't got a chance. No one's going to believe you. No one really believes in monsters.'

Daniel looked up at the trees and raised his hands. He pointed to a small clearing ahead of the climbing frame. As the trees rustled, hundreds, if not thousands of birds shot out into the air. Branches, twigs and clumps of grass in their beaks. All shapes and sizes.

'Tastes.....old!' said Daniel, as he flipped open the book and licked his fingers. He turned to Tim's mum, 'it tastes positively *disgusting*.'

As the birds swooped down to the small clearing, they opened their dirty, crooked beaks and let the twigs and branches fall to the ground. As more and more birds opened their beaks, a pile formed on the bed of the forest.

The sound from hundreds of birds flapping their wings was deafening. Tim didn't know where to look as his line of sight was blinded by flashes of brown, yellow and black. He blinked again. What was wrong with his eyes? Was he seeing things?

Daniel approached the mound of branches, as Goth Boy pushed Tim's mum forward.

'No more secrets,' said Daniel as he ripped out a page at random, and used his teeth to tear it apart. He spat the pieces out over the mound of wood.

'No, you can't!' shouted Tim.

'Oh, but I can. That's just it, Tim-o-thee. I can. You simply couldn't leave it where it was, could you. You really think I'm going to let it be exposed. No, no. I've got something altogether different in mind.'

Daniel continued to tear pages out of the book. He screwed some up into balls and others into pieces, all the time making the pile higher and higher. 'You don't happen to have a light, do you?'

Tim frowned.

'Well, what do you know,' said Daniel, flicking his thumb over his forefinger. A strong flame rose high into the air. He tugged a page from the middle of the book and lit one end, waving it in the air.

The flame roared out. Tim felt the heat on his face.

With a look of intense satisfaction Daniel dropped the flaming paper onto to the mound below – instantly igniting the wood pile into a raging fire.

Daniel looked at the book, 'like most things in life. All good things simply *must* come to an end,' and with that, he threw the book on top of the bonfire and laughed as it curled and twisted under the heat.

Tim caught Gemma's eyes and nodded. He sprang forwards, pushed Goth Boy to the ground and grabbed his mum's hands. He pulled her with him and they sprinted ahead of the fire, beyond the climbing frame.

'Get them!' shouted Daniel, as he waved his hands in the air towards his birds.

For a moment Tim's mum tried to free her mouth.

'It's just going to slow us down Mum, later.'

They ran through the forest at a furious pace, dodging broken tree trunks and all manner of trees and skinny, bone-like bushes that sprang up in front of them, breaking their passage.

Daniel was first to sprint after them. He threw his arm out to his left at an angle, forcing a wave of birds to rise above the trees and charge towards the escapees. A few more steps and he thrust his arm out to his right and repeated the action – sending another wave of birds in pursuit from the other side.

'There's nowhere to run,' shouted Goth Boy. 'You're on our turf now.'

The trees became denser, slowing down the birds flight. Some birds smashed against trees and plunged to the ground – twitching on the forest floor. Others got their wings sliced off between thick overhanging branches – gushes of purple and red oozed out of their obese bodies.

Daniel sprinted in pursuit. His fists clenched. Mouth foaming. He was getting closer.

Tim narrowly missed a branch that was sticking out, only to have another rip against his cheek and slice the top layer of skin off. He screamed out.

Gemma tripped and for the briefest of moments lost her balance, before regaining it and increasing speed, her handbag bashing against her back ferociously as she tried to ignore the pain.

Evergreen bushes got closer and closer together. Like walls of a maze. The ground dipped, and all three of them splashed through a stream before returning to higher ground. They reached another small clearing.

For a moment, Daniel and Goth Boy couldn't be seen.

Tim came to a stop and reached into his pocket for the compass.

Through the trees, Gemma was first to see the lake through a small gap.

All three rested by a large oak tree, out of breath, panting heavily.

'We've....got...to...open the box,' said Tim. 'It's our only way out of here. Quick, Gemma, give me the box.'

Gemma nodded, wiped the sweat from her brow and began to reach for her handbag.

'I'll get it, Tim,' she said.

Tim's mum seized the chance to rip the cord around her mouth. She spat out a sickly greenish gunk and wiped her hand across her face. 'That's disgusting,' she said.

Tim pulled out the compass. Just as he was about to open the lid, a bird swooped over his palm and knocked the compass to the ground, forcing it to roll under a fallen tree trunk ahead.

'Don't worry, Tim. Everything's going to be fine,' said Tim's mum.

Tim scratched his head as his mum winked at him. Then he felt a sharp pain in his leg and immediately fell to the ground.

'Tim!' said his mum.

'My leg, Mum, my leg,' said Tim clasping it, 'one of the birds. I think it got me.'

Daniel and Goth Boy appeared from behind adjacent trees.

Daniel's army of birds surrounded them in a circle. They spun repeatedly in the same circular pattern like vultures.

'Gemma, your nearest - the compass, you've got to get it quick!' said Tim.

'Get her,' said Daniel, pointing towards Tim's mum.

'No!' shouted Tim, looking desperately at Gemma.

Goth Boy sprinted across the forest bed towards Tim's mum as Gemma ran to the tree trunk.

Tim felt like everything was happening in slow motion as his mum took a deep breath, and held back her head.

Music burst from her lungs and filled the air with the most exquisite tones. Tones like Tim had never heard before. Tones that tore at the flesh of the birds and forced them violently down to the ground. They smashed into branches. Beaks exploded.

Gemma turned to look, in shock, as a whole wing ripped off of one of the birds and narrowly missed her head. She reached under the tree trunk and desperately felt for the compass. Until she felt the cold metal against her finger tips.

Tim turned to Daniel. For the first time, Tim could see a change in him. A tortured expression. A heady mix of fear and pain.

Daniel covered his ears and screamed out loud, like he was being deafened at a rock concert.

Tim looked up. Coloured ribbons sprayed from all corners of the sky. Different shapes and sizes. It was like a firework show as the air filled with the sound of his mum singing an old Celtic-like song. He couldn't understand the words. Ancient sounding words. Haunting words. Rich, warm melodies. Like a thick blanket of hope being shaken over the forest.

Tim remembered the kaleidoscope. He recalled the dancing, animated images in the kaleidoscope from the old man in the TV. The way it melted on his bed. Those were the colours he was seeing. The kaleidoscope - it was a sign.

Daniel gripped his ears tightly and shouted out to the remaining birds. 'Defence formation. Defend me!'

A group of birds flocked around Daniel, their wings entwined, forming a barrier between Daniel and Tim's mum, like a protective shield. Holding one of the bird's legs, Daniel ran with the shield towards Gemma – his eyes darkening – becoming blacker...and blacker.

Goth Boy pulled his hands away from his ears, tore a large branch from a tree and threw it with all his strength towards Tim's mum, knocking her to the ground.

Tim turned to his mum as the Celtic tones stopped. The coloured ribbons disappeared in front of his eyes. He rushed to his mum's side, and held her head. 'Look out, Gemma, Daniel...'

Gemma put the compass in her bag and picked up a loose branch. She bashed it into Daniel's side, avoiding his shield.

'Gemma, the compass. Open it. Remember what it did to the birds on the courtyard. Open it quick!'

Daniel threw his shield into the air and the birds spread out, circling around Gemma.

'The button, it won't press....I can't....open it,' she said.

'Keep trying, keep trying,' said Tim, waving birds away as they swooped down close to his mum.

Gemma sprinted closer to Tim, pressing the button on the compass, looking over her shoulder as Daniel pushed a bird into her back. The bird smacked into her handbag, knocking her over and the rosewood box fell out and spun into the air.

Goth Boy jumped up onto the tree above him and transformed into a bird. He plunged down to the spot where Tim was stroking his mum's head.

His mum opened her eyes and blinked.

Gemma screamed, 'Tim, catch the box!'

Tim reached his hands out as the box hurtled towards him.

Gemma was able to break her fall with her arms as her legs spun around and hit Tim's side, just as he caught the box.

Tim tried not to lose his grip on the box.

Goth Boy's bird-like form was just inches from Tim's head.

'Pass me the compass, quickly!' said Tim.

Gemma found the compass in the undergrowth and pressed it into Tim's hand.

Tim pressed the button.

Nothing.

He looked straight up, above the forest, to a high place. 'Give me strength,' he muttered and tried the button again. 'It can't be broken. It just can't.'

The compass lid jerked.

It tilted open.

He attached the compass to the grooves on the box. A bright light burst out of the box as it opened. The light shot out straight towards Goth Boy's bird-like form.

Gemma screamed. 'Look, Tim, the Goth.'

As the light engulfed Goth Boy, his whole body was sprayed with fire, as one wing turned back into an arm – the other wing burst into flames. Feathers burning.

The smell was like burning rubber. It was foul.

As the Goth hit a branch, his entire body burst into a ball of flames, forcing the tree to catch fire.

'No!!!' said Daniel, as he made a fist in the air.

Tim saw Daniel's arm reach towards him as the forest began to blur.

He held his mum tightly, as Gemma gripped Tim's shoulder.

All Tim could see was a rainbow of colours as he lost the feeling in his hands, then his legs. Reality was disappearing.

Sight. Sound. Feeling.

Gone.

The forest faded into a distant memory.

CHAPTER EIGHTEEN

Tim opened his eyes first, finding his mum still lying on his lap.

'We're safe Mum. We're out of the forest,' he said.

'Where are we? What just happened?' said Tim's mum.

'I'm not really sure where we are,' said Tim, looking around the brightly lit room. 'This isn't what I was expecting.' He gripped his mum's hand tight. 'Are you feeling okay?'

She squeezed his hand. 'Apart from my legs. It feels like they've gone to sleep. I still can't believe you're here. I thought I'd never see you again.' A tear fell down her cheek.

'Hey, Mum, don't cry. Everything's going to be okay.'

Tim surveyed the room. A bright, vertical light shone from top to bottom across the centre of the room. The light adjusted its position, like a giant spirit level, reflecting on the shiny floor. As it pulsated, ripples of colour jumped up and down at random. It was like a thin partitioned wall made of light and colour that shimmered and glowed. This couldn't be real. It just *couldn't* be.

A row of monitors hovered in the middle of the room, as if floating in mid-air.

'Look at these monitors,' said Tim.

One of the monitors showed a man's hands gripping the handlebars of a motorbike. It felt like a first person shooter game, without the shooter. As the bike raced down the street it hit a car bonnet and Tim felt himself flying over the bonnet – experiencing whatever happened to this motorcyclist.

Gemma's eyes opened wider than wide. She blinked continuously. 'Where....what...,' she blinked again. 'Hey, this isn't right. This isn't the seventeenth century. Where are we?'

Tim shrugged. 'Remember what you said last time we opened the box. It's like it was linked with the book,' he said.

'Except this time, we don't have the book. The book's gone,' said Gemma, frowning.

'Exactly. So who knows where we are,' said Tim. He brushed his hand over his face, up and down and stretched to one of the monitors. 'Where are the wires?' he said, '....and..the power....where's the electric cable?' He passed the monitors and observed the sheet of light that ran through the centre of the room.

'Do you think we're dead? Is this....heaven? It's so white in here,' said Tim.

'It's like we're in the future,' said Gemma. 'Look, there's just static on these monitors,' she said. 'Did you see anything?'

'Yes, before you came round, I saw these pictures. Well, not pictures, it was more like a movie or something. Someone getting knocked off a motorbike. It felt like I was him.'

'Weird. What do you think it means? Where are we?'

Tim knocked his hands on the walls. 'It's solid, listen.'

'No windows, no doors. What kind of place is this?' said Gemma. 'I'm starting to feel like Alice in Wonderland. What's next, a Cheshire cat?' she said, turning to Tim's mum. 'Are you okay, Mrs Shaw?'

'I'm fine. Just call me Claire.'

Gemma stroked her hand. 'I can't imagine what you've been through.'

Tim turned to the monitor. 'Look, the static. It's gone. It's getting clearer. Looks like a hospital. There's a heart monitor, see.'

Tim's mum and Gemma turned to the monitor as its picture came into focus.

'Whoever it is, he's lying in bed. It's like we're seeing things through the eyes of the patient,' said Tim.

'The image is getting a bit blurry now. Someone's sitting down next to him look. He's turning his head.'

'Oh God! Look. It's Daniel,' said Tim.

Tim's mum gripped his hand tight.

'It's okay Mum, he can't see you.'

'What's he doing?' said Gemma.

'Daniel's holding this guy's hand,' said Tim.

'You think he's a relative?' said Gemma.

Tim's mum frowned.

'Hardly, look how tight he's squeezing it,' said Tim. 'That's not a comforting grip, look at the expression on Daniel's face. It looks like he's getting a high from it. Like he's on drugs or something.'

'Mum, are you okay?' said Tim. 'You've gone all pale.'

'Wait, look, nurses, they're taking him away,' said Gemma.

'Look, it's getting all blurry. Daniel's face, it's fading...,' said Tim.

'Like the guy's eyes are shutting.'

'I think he's dying Gemma.'

'What's Daniel doing there?'

Tim shrugged. 'The monitor it's gone all black.'

'You think?' said Gemma.

'Yes, Gemma,' said Tim's mum. 'He's dead.'

Out of the pulsating light in the middle of the room, a figure rose up from a hole in the ground.

'Hey, where did you come from?' said Tim.

'Look, it's him,' said Gemma.

'The postman!' said Tim.

'You?' said Tim's mum.

'Yes, Claire. It's been a long time,' said the postman.

Tim stared at his mum, 'you *know* him?'

'Oh yes, I know him.'

'Who are you? I mean, who are you really?' said Tim, turning to the postman.

'He's a Seeker, Tim,' said Tim's mum.

'A Seeker?'

'People like us Tim, people with gifts. The fight with the Deceivers. It goes back centuries. The Seekers. They're on our side. They want to help us.'

'You see, you and your mum. Well, you have a condition,' said the postman.

'A condition? You mean a gift?'

'Yes, something unique. Something that affects just a small percentage of the population.'

'You're talking about my painting? The way it makes people feel?' said Tim.

'That's one of your gifts, Tim,' said the postman.

'One of them? You mean I have more?' said Tim, scratching his head.

The postman nodded.

Tim pondered on the firework display he witnessed as his mum sang. The flashes of light. 'The colours. The colours I see?'

'Yes, Tim. The colours. You see colours when you hear some sounds, don't you?'

Tim nodded, 'I do now...but I never used to.'

'It's called synaesthesia, Tim. The condition we have,' said his mum.

'Sinners-what? What on earth is that?' said Gemma.

The postman nodded towards one of the monitors.

Tim looked up, his mouth open. 'Is that Wikipedia?' He turned to the monitor and read out the Wikipedia entry:

"Synaesthesia from the ancient Greek (syn), "together" and (aisthesis), "sensation", is a neurological condition in which stimulation of one sensory or cognitive pathway leads to automatic, involuntary experiences in a second sensory or cognitive pathway...."

'So you see Tim, you're special,' said the postman. 'You've just unlocked the ability to turn sound into colours. Colours that only you can see, and others like you. Your other gift - the ability to turn the images you create into a form of positive energy that can be *felt* by others. It means your condition isn't limited to one pathway. You see, both you and your mum have an emerging strand. What we're calling "projective synaesthesia". Because you can convert the experience for others to see. To feel.'

'That's awesome,' said Gemma. 'It's like you're a super hero or something. And Tim's mum?'

'Her voice?' said Tim, 'it was her voice wasn't it? That's what was killing the birds. In the forest.'

The postman nodded. 'Your mum, Tim, has a really unique ability. Her voice transforms into a positive force. An energy if you like. It repels the Deceivers. Repels them like nothing we've ever seen before.'

'That's why they took her away?' said Tim.

'Yes, Tim. Her gift is a real threat.'

Gemma slapped her forehead. 'That's why they kept her in a sound-proof room.'

'And why they gagged her,' Tim continued.

The postman nodded. 'You see, the Deceivers. They live off of the negative elements of life.'

'Yes, we kind of figured that out,' said Tim, looking at Gemma.

'This is amazing. Projective synaes...thesia you called it,' said Tim. 'I can hardly pronounce it, let alone understand it.' He remembered the book and frowned, turning to the postman. 'But the book. Daniel. He destroyed it.'

'Yes Tim, I know.'

'You don't look too disappointed. I mean, the Deceivers got what they wanted.'

'It's not the end of the world. Remember, the formula isn't a secret anymore. It's a minor setback for us. Daniel has lost the boy.'

'The Goth?'

'Yes, as you call him. He was destroyed by the light. The light from the box.'

The monitor filled with an image of Professor Laws.

'Our top priority now is to protect the professor,' said the postman.

'So all of this. I mean everything that's happened. It's all to stop the Deceivers from destroying all the good in the world?' said Gemma.

'That's one way of looking at it, Gemma,' said the postman. 'They know that if man can reverse the effects of social decay, they will lose. You see, Deceivers feed on negative energy. On the evil that people do.'

'The man on the motorbike,' said Tim. 'That's what Daniel was doing. Feeding?'

Tim's mum took his hand and nodded.

'That's why you went all white, Mum? You knew?'

Tim's mum nodded. 'Yes, Tim. Before Daniel kidnapped me, I was helping the Seekers. I've known about the Deceivers for some time.'

'But you never mentioned it. Not to me. Not to Dad?'

'What do you think your dad would say about all this?'

Tim smiled. 'He'd say it was all a load of nonsense.'

'Exactly,' said Tim's mum.

'So why didn't they just, you know, kill you. I mean, why did they kidnap you?' said Tim.

'Imagine what would be unleashed from a synaesthete if they were to die,' said the postman. 'What kind of positive force do you think that would unleash? All that energy has to go somewhere. That's what the Deceivers are afraid of.'

Tim scratched his head. 'So how many types of synaesthesia are there?'

'Over sixty variations,' said the postman.

'Awesome!' said Gemma. 'I think I remember seeing a documentary about it. Like super heroes, but with real powers!'

Tim looked at the monitors, then at the postman. 'So what is it exactly you do here, what are these monitors for? Why are you called Seekers?'

'This is what we call room 57. It's where we inspect.'

'Inspect? Inspect what?'

'Dreams and experiences, mostly.'

'Dreams? You can inspect dreams?'

'Yes, Tim. How did you think we knew you were ready?'

'Ready for what?' said Tim, scratching his head.

'I said it all started with your dream, Tim,' said Gemma. 'I was right.'

'The clarity in your dream, Tim, was a sign,' said the postman. 'A sign you were ready. A sign your gift was fully developed. That's when I knew you were ready. Ready to help find your mum. Any earlier, with your gift undeveloped, well...you would have been easy prey for the Deceivers. They would have killed you.'

'But why didn't you just tell me? Why did you have to send me the compass?'

'It wasn't an easy decision, Tim. Seekers have remained a secret for centuries. Fighting against the Deceivers with help from synaesthetes. Can you imagine how you would have reacted if I'd told you about us? The Deceivers – men who turn into birds, your gift, your mum's gift, the end of all goodness in the world? You simply wouldn't have believed it. That's why I sent you the compass, to help you. To protect you. To guide you here. I saw the book in your dream, you see. It wasn't possible to see where it was, but I knew it was the book.'

Gemma interrupted. 'So Daniel. The Deceivers. They can see dreams too? They saw the book? That's why they came after Tim?'

The postman nodded. 'Yes, they knew Tim would find the book, eventually, just as we did.'

'But even I couldn't remember a book in my dream,' said Tim.

'Don't you remember the bookcase in the library?' said the postman. 'A book fell on the floor, from the bookcase, remember?'

'Sort of...I remembered the library when we were at the college, after Gemma mentioned her school trip. That's what reminded me...you know, about my dream. I didn't remember the book though, not until the bird in the library; it tore the page out of the book, just like it did in my dream. That's when I remembered the book.'

'Hey, you never told me that you dreamed that!' said Gemma.

'Sorry, Gemma. These flashbacks...they've been happening all the time. It's almost like I was seeing the future. I mean, you've heard of deja vu, this was like deja vu on steroids!' Tim frowned.

'What is it, Tim?' said Gemma.

Tim turned to the postman. 'Why didn't you just get the book yourself then, if you saw it in my dream?' he said.

'It's not always that simple,' said the postman. 'Like all dreams, they are...let's say distorted. Not everything appears exactly as it does in the real world. You probably can't remember seeing anything like Trinity College in your dream, right?'

'That's right,' said Tim. 'Some things were similar, but not identical. I don't remember any arched windows.'

'So, you see,' said the postman, 'because we didn't know where the book was...well, that's why you had to discover it yourself.'

'Why weren't you able to help find Claire earlier, though. Why did you wait a whole year?' said Gemma.

'We couldn't find her. We tried. Wherever they locked her away, it was off the radar for us. If we'd have come for you Tim, when your mum went missing, it would have been very dangerous. The Deceivers may have found you. They can track us. With your gift still undeveloped...well I think you understand what I'm saying. The risk was too high.'

'But the text messages. If you sent them, how did you know I'd find out about mum? I mean, you never did come and tell me what happened.'

'It was a bit of a gamble, Tim. We knew that Daniel would track you down. If he could see what we did, in your dream, he knew the risk. We believed that eventually he would make a mistake. You had the bargaining chip. You had the book. And that's what you figured out when you offered Daniel the trade. Because your gift was developed, Daniel couldn't kill you. Just like he couldn't kill your mum. That's why we took the gamble.'

'And the kaleidoscope,' said Gemma. 'You gave it to Tim, to show him his gift, right?'

The postman nodded, turning to Tim. 'We wanted you to understand. To feel it for yourself. Like I said, we knew you probably wouldn't believe us if we told you. So experiencing it for yourself, well...it was to prepare you.'

'And when the kaleidoscope melted on my bed. It was a sign?' said Tim. 'I remember when I saw mum sing. The colours. The way they bounced. It was just like the kaleidoscope melting on my bed. Like you were showing me what mum's gift would do. Like you were showing me my other gift – what I'd see when I hear sounds.'

'Yes, Tim. I see you've understood well,' said the postman.

'What about the wooden box though?' said Gemma, pointing at the rosewood box. 'It took us back in time. To the seventeenth century.'

'Yes and no, Gemma,' said the postman. 'You see, these boxes are the only gateway to room 57. It's like a security measure we take. To stop the Deceivers from finding us here. The boxes are buried in different parts of your Earth.'

'But the box, it did take us to the seventeenth century. We were there,' said Tim. 'We saw it. We smelt it. We felt it.'

'Not exactly, Tim. You see it was this room. Room 57. It drew on the *life* of the book. The book that Edward Noble wrote. The room recreated 17th century Cambridge for you. Where the book started its life.'

'You're saying the box brought us to *this* room? This room can recreate a whole street? A whole prison?' said Tim.

The postman nodded.

'No way, that's crazy!' said Tim.

'And when we saw Edward later? He was older, like we moved forwards in time,' said Gemma.

'When I dropped the book,' said Tim. 'It flipped open, near the end of the book. That's what made it happen?' he said, glancing at the postman.

'Yes, Tim, if the pages went forward, so did you. Like I said, the room drew on the life of the book. Humans aren't the only ones who experience life.'

Gemma nudged Tim. 'Yes, books have feelings too, you know!'

'But it can't be. This room's...well, not big enough,' said Tim.

'Just as with your Dali, not everything is as it seems,' said the postman, winking at Gemma, before he nodded towards the walls.

'Tim, what's happening?' said Gemma, as the walls started to open out and fold back on themselves. The walls flopped backwards, over and over again, expanding the space until it felt like they were stood on a giant football pitch.

The white walls of the room were replaced with familiar paintings as the walls drew in, enclosing them in a small room, no bigger than twelve square metres.

A desk. A bed. An encyclopedia on the floor.

'It's my bedroom!' said Tim.

'All this...it's part of this room fifty seven?' said Tim.

'Yes, Tim, that's what I'm trying to tell you,' said the postman.

'That's why no one could see us, hear us. In Edward's study. In the Spinning House. Because we weren't really there?' said Tim.

The postman nodded, as the room restored to its natural state of pulsating lights and monitors hovering in the air.

'And the experiences, you said dreams *and* experiences?' said Tim.

'That's a long story, Tim, best kept for another day.'

'Do you know?' said Tim, turning to his mum.

His mum shrugged.

Tim rubbed his chin. 'I'm not letting this one go. So...we were in my bedroom, because I've experienced it. Because I'm connected to it. Like the book was connected to Edward. To the time he was writing it in?'

'Yes, something like that,' said the postman.

'So that's what you mean about experiences...,' said Tim.

'Well, that's a part of it,' said the postman. 'Here, take this.'

Tim took a black plastic-like device from the postman and turned it over. 'Hey, that's my TV remote!'

Tim looked at the remote, then up at the central monitor, getting a nod from the postman. He pressed the "on" button and watched the monitor fade in.

'What's that?' said Tim's mum, pointing at the screen.

'Wait a minute,' said Tim, scratching his head. 'That's....but it can't be...'

'What, Tim, what is it?' said Gemma.

Tim's grey matter felt like it was doing overtime. Looking up at the monitor he could see bodies floating in a thick, muddy water. Animals. Bedsheets. Gushing down what clearly used to be a road, as the helicopter flew from the street to a tumbled down shack.

'Currys. The man in the TV. It really *was* you,' said Tim, turning to the postman.

The postman frowned.

'What are you talking about, Tim?' said Gemma.

'After I got the kaleidoscope, when everything went back to normal. There was a newsflash on TV. A flood. Somewhere in India I think. This is the same programme I saw in the shop.'

'What does it mean?' said Tim. 'What's this got to do with experiences?'

Tim's mum took his arm and gripped it tight. 'Tim, everything that happens in this world. Well, it has consequences.'

'You mean, you *know*?'

'Yes, Tim. Remember what he said earlier. About why Daniel couldn't kill us?'

'Something about an energy being released when you die,' said Tim.

Gemma's eyes shot wide open.

'Gemma?' said Tim.

'All these people in the water,' said Gemma. 'All dead. You mean something happens? An energy is released when they die, too?'

'Like the man on the motorbike?' said Tim. 'His memories?'

'No. It's not memories,' said Gemma. 'It's their experiences isn't it? You mean...something gets released. Even from them?'

'Well, that too....but that's not what I'm trying to say,' said Tim's mum.

'What do you mean then?' said Tim.

'How can I explain?' said Tim's mum. 'Look, Tim, you remember that movie you used to like. The one with Ashton Kutcher?'

'Oh, I like him,' said Gemma. 'You mean "Valentine's Day"?'

'No...come on!' said Tim. 'She means "Butterfly Effect".'

'Yes, yes, "Butterfly Effect",' said Tim's mum. 'There are always consequences. Everything we do has consequences. A turn left. A turn right. Every decision we make has an impact.'

'But what's that got to do with it? I mean, what are you trying to say?' said Gemma.

'When you experience something good, something bad, it's...well...stored. Somehow. When we die, it gets released.'

'Released where?' said Gemma.

'Everywhere,' said Tim's mum. 'Like an invisible soup, washing over everything.'

'I think I get why you said it was going to be a long story now,' said Tim, turning to the postman with a smirk.

'What your mum is really trying to say,' said the postman, 'is that everything you do, in life...it has consequences. Your experiences, if you like, well...they're released back into the world. An energy, a life-force. It's what the very fabric of the universe is built on.'

'You mean, something like our souls?' said Gemma.

The postman nodded. 'That's one way of looking at it, yes.'

'So what are you trying to say?' said Tim.

'You said "Butterfly Effect",' said Gemma, turning to Tim's mum.

'You mean this flood?' said Tim. 'This flood is related to *other* people dying?'

'Not just people dying, Tim. Bad people,' said Tim's mum.

'Even normal people?' said Gemma. 'I mean those who don't have Tim's gift. Synaesthesia.'

The postman nodded.

'So the bad experiences,' said Tim. 'The bad things people do....you mean they can influence floods? Natural disasters?'

The postman nodded. 'In exceptional circumstances. Especially in recent times.'

A monitor next to the central one fizzled and refocussed.

'Aren't they the Twin towers?' said Gemma.

The postman frowned.

'You mean...all this terrorism. It can do this?' said Tim, looking at the images of gushing water on the central monitor.

Tim looked down as images of the flood faded away. He felt his mum's hand squeeze his arm tighter. Her face solemn.

'Achoo!' Gemma put her hand to her face, 'sorry..'

Tim slapped his forehead. 'I've just remembered. Gemma,' he said. 'When we were in the library, after Edward hid the book, he sang a nursery rhyme. It's been bugging me ever since, why he sang "Ring-a-ring of roses".'

Tim turned to the postman.

'That nursery rhyme,' said Tim. 'It couldn't have existed then, could it? It was strange enough that he sang it in the first place. But I just remember thinking, it can't be that old. How could he possibly know that rhyme if he was really living in the seventeenth century?'

The postman turned to the monitor as the nursery rhyme came up and the words filled the room. Then came the voices. Children. No older than six or seven.

'Ring-a-ring of roses,
A pocketful of posies,
Attischo, Attischo,
We all fall down.'

Tim saw dark colours dancing ominously, blacks, deep, dark and bloody reds.

'What you have to understand about that nursery rhyme,' said the postman, 'is that it was a rhyme born out of the Great Plague. The Great Plague of 1665.'

Gemma raised her eyebrows. 'Remember what the professor found in the book, Tim? He told us about the Great Plague.'

Tim nodded. 'And that meant something to Edward Noble?' said Tim. 'Surely he wasn't even born?'

'You're right, Tim, he wasn't born then.' said the postman. 'But it did mean something to him. A great deal actually. You see, back in 1665 the university had to be shut down for two years. The Great Plague had spread to other parts of the country and reached as far as Cambridge. This was a time that disturbed Edward's family greatly, having lost several family members in the ferociously hot summer of that year. Edward had never understood how something so dark, so malevolent could execute with such ferocity and swiftness in such a short space of time. It was an epidemic that wiped out tens of thousands of people – first spreading a series of circular red blotches on the victims skin, before the poor victims would enter a fit of sneezing. Death would follow shortly afterwards. That's what the nursery rhyme is all about you see. Even though Edward himself wasn't born, events of those years had left a permanent mark on his family. A mark that would shape the nature of his future study. A mark that ultimately led to him being in the library that very night. You see, the nursery rhyme at school had brought him such sadness.'

Tim sighed. 'Poor guy,' said Tim. 'Hey, what was that noise?' He turned as tiny white dots floated in front of him.

A sound like an untuned television filled the room.

Tim turned to the monitor. It was blurred, fuzzy, like something was interfering with the reception. As the picture on the monitor became clearer, Tim saw the familiar sight of the coffee shop in Cambridge – a man sat alone at one of the tables dressed in a Santa Claus outfit.

CHAPTER NINETEEN

Santa held a single piece of paper in his hand with a torn, perforated edge. He turned to the radio that was playing and fixed his gaze on the channel dial. No one else in the coffee shop seemed to notice as the channel flipped and the music changed.

As "Santa Claus is coming to town" played over the radio waves, Santa lit a cigarette. People around him started to fidget. He reached inside his coat and pulled out a pocket watch. It was stained, with traces of what looked like black ink on the silver, back casing. The glass front was slightly frosted, but still clear enough to make out the hour hand as it hit twelve.

He looked around the coffee shop at the sad and lonely faces and laughed. His laughter soon turned into a deep and hearty cough that disturbed the rest of the punters. It was no regular cough. This was a cough born in a dark place. A place far, far away. A place where the light didn't shine. He lifted the piece of paper up towards the light. Words on both sides. Small letters. Scruffy. Untidy. Scribbled by the author in a hurry.

Santa stared at the words on the paper – his cough subsiding into an evil grin as he pulled the paper to his cigarette and watched it catch fire.

≕⊹ ⊹≕

'Daniel!' shouted Tim. 'It's Daniel.'

'Yes, Tim, I'm afraid so,' said the postman.

'You've gone all white, Tim, what's wrong?' said Gemma.

'It's that song. I heard it in my dream. It's like it was calling out to me,' said Tim, as an animated Santa display in a toy shop window came into his head. 'Be good for goodness sake. The words in the song. It's like the clue was there from the very start. That's really what this is all about, isn't it? If we're not good....that's it...I mean, they win don't they?'

'Yes, Tim. You see, the Deceivers believe they have to destroy *all* goodness,' said the postman. 'The more goodness there is in the world, the weaker it makes them. As Edward discovered, social decay was already on a path. A path to a logical end. All the Deceivers have been trying to do is help it along. Accelerate it.'

Gemma turned to the postman, looking at the burning paper in Daniel's hand. 'Is that what I think it is? The proof. The proof of the formula. The page the bird ripped out....in the library?'

The postman nodded and switched off the monitor.

'So it *was* Daniel, in the library?' said Tim.

'Yes, Tim. Ever since you discovered the book, Daniel and his kind have been trying to destroy it. You see, as long as it was hidden in the library it wasn't a threat to them. But once you found it. Well, the possibility of people studying it. With all the advancements made these last three hundred years. Understanding it. The risk was too high.'

Tim looked down.

'What is it Tim?' asked Gemma.

'Well they've won, haven't they? I mean, the whole book, it's all destroyed now. The formulas, the proof, everything.'

'As long as we have synaesthetes,' said the postman, 'like Claire and you, Tim, we have a fighting chance. And remember, Professor Laws has also seen the formula. So it's not a secret now.'

'Synaesthetes. Plural? You mean there are more?' said Gemma.

'Oh, yes,' said the postman, turning to one of the monitors, 'like I said, it's a condition that affects a small percentage of the population.'

'Awesome!' said Gemma, looking up at the monitor as tiny dots scattered all over the Earth. 'So synaesthetes, they're really all over the world?'

Tim's mum turned to Gemma, glancing at the monitor. 'Yes, Gemma.'

'Gemma, do you remember what you said in art club?' said Tim. 'You know, about monsters.'

'I think I said something like they don't exist,' she said. 'I said there was an explanation for everything.'

'And what do you think now, then?' said Tim.

'I don't know what to think anymore. It's like my whole world has been turned upside down. Like...I have to believe the impossible. It's like all fantasy. Everything I've seen in the movies. Time travel, monsters, magic. It's all real. A secret society that's existed for centuries trying to destroy goodness. I couldn't have imagined that. I don't even think Dali could have imagined that. I mean, I haven't even seen a movie about it. Read a book about it. It just sounds *impossible*.'

'What is it, Tim?' said the postman. 'You look troubled.'

'I was thinking about what Gemma just said. Impossible. I still don't get how my painting had a map inside it. You know, the map that lead to the book in the library. Now that's impossible. It doesn't make sense that I could have known about the book. Is that part of my gift too?'

'But remember Tim, you said yourself that you saw the library in your dream. The book too,' said Gemma.

'I know, but how could I know it was in Trinity College? In the library? How could the map be hidden in my painting? I didn't do it!'

Gemma shrugged. 'Maybe we'll never know. There's not a rational explanation for everything after all.' She sighed.

'Why are you looking at me like that?' said Tim, observing the know-it-all expression on the postman's face.

'That might not be true....in this case. You see, I suspect it's related to your gift in some way,' said the postman. 'But perhaps more importantly with,' the postman paused, '...your ancestry.'

'Ancestry? What do you mean?'

'What I mean is, Edward Noble,' said the postman, as an image of Edward appeared on one of the monitors.

'He was your great, great, great, great, *great* grandfather,' said the postman.

Tim turned to the postman then to the monitor and scratched his head, his mouth wide open.

'On your mother's side,' said the postman, with a smile.

ABOUT THE AUTHOR

 JONATHAN WHITE is a father to two beautiful children, technologist, entrepreneur, author and real estate investor. Born and raised in the UK, he's an adventurer at heart – having lived & worked for many years in Malaysia, Bulgaria and Estonia. *The Secret on the Second Shelf* is his debut children's novel.

Printed in Great Britain
by Amazon